DAURA

DAURA

A Novel

Anukrti Upadhyay

FOURTH ESTATE • *New Delhi*

First published in India in 2019 by Fourth Estate
An imprint of HarperCollins Publishers
HarperCollins *Publishers* India, Cyber City, Building 10-A, Gurugram, Haryana-122002, India
www.harpercollins.co.in

2 4 6 8 10 9 7 5 3 1

P-ISBN: 9789353570019

Typeset in 10.5/16.3 Scala at
Manipal Digital Systems, Manipal

Printed and bound at
Manipal Technologies Limited, Manipal

*

HarperCollins *Publishers*, Macken House, 39/40 Mayor Street Upper, Dublin 1, D01 C9W8, Ireland

To my family,
with love and gratitude

EXCERPTS FROM
THE CONFIDENTIAL REPORT ON
THE COLLECTOR
OF ___ DISTRICT, RAJASTHAN

I

THE ORDERLY'S TALE

I REMEMBER THE FIRST TIME we arrived here at the dak bangla. Dusk had fallen, but there was just enough light to confirm my suspicion – that Saheb had brought us to yet another burning, godforsaken wilderness in the desert's entrails. I have been on enough district tours in my years with Saheb to know these places from miles away. They all follow the same pattern – unending sand dunes, scattered dhanis, and seedy dak banglas like this one. One look around, and you know that you are alone with the deadly desert. I have seen too many of these dak banglas and spent too many evenings and nights in dusty rooms, sweating, swatting mosquitoes and cursing my fate...

I am not unreasonable, Sir, I don't expect to be in Jaipur or Ajmer every day, but anyone would agree that to spend twenty-five days out of thirty in sandpits like these, like a godless goh lizard, is excessive. A young man needs to go out once in a while with his mates, watch a movie, have a few drinks, that kind of thing. Instead, in these places, after ironing Saheb's clothes and making his bed and arranging his papers and arguing with the cook over his meals, I have nothing to do but stare at the piles of sand and the wall of sky. I have noticed a strange thing: the sky seems solid and close when you are out here in the desert, like it wants to shut you in forever. You may think me odd, Sir, but watching the burning dunes by day and listening to the sand screeching in the open desert at night would make anyone odd.

True, though we are far from the headquarters and in the middle of this dustbowl desert, it's not as if there is no one around. There is staff at the dak bangla, and any number of tribesmen from neighbouring dhanis. I could always join them for a game of chaupad or cards, chit-chat, go out and have some local brew. They would be glad enough to have someone like me to talk to. And Saheb won't mind either – he likes to mingle with them himself. Now, I don't mind talking to or passing the time occasionally with the folk here, but I can't mix with them regularly.

Why? Well, for one, they are very ignorant. Most of them haven't been as far as the headquarters, let alone Jaipur. Besides, all they can think of is goats and camels and silly old stories. Even the staff of the dak bangla are illiterate, mere servants hired locally from among the Banjaras, and

I am a government employee – orderly to the Collector. The Additional District Magistrates and Saheb's Sub-Divisional Magistrate, who would not look at the riffraff around here, call me by my name and ask after my health. Too much familiarity with the desert folk is hardly appropriate for someone like me. I, at all events, try to maintain the decorum of Saheb's position.

Yes, I realize I am digressing, I apologize for it. So, to go back to when we first arrived here: the dak bangla looked then as it does now – old, all colour burnt out of it by the sun so you can't tell whether it was always this bleached-bone, old-carcass white. True, the veranda is deep and the rooms are large and numerous, but what is there in the desert except space? And you can see for yourself how wide all the windows are, and completely unshaded against the sun. Though there are new electric fans in the rooms, there are no coolers and the veranda still has an old, tattered, hand-pulled fan. The broiling heat of the day would make this place as hot as a griddle on a mud chulha if I didn't keep the staff here on their toes and make them spray water on the reed-blinds four times a day. Saheb, of course, likes this old place very much, much more than his comfortable bungalow at the headquarters ... but that is how Saheb is. He has an odd liking for queer places, uncouth people. If he didn't, would he choose to be buried in this place instead of staying peacefully at the headquarters like other sahebs?

I am not saying there is anything wrong with my Collector Saheb. If he prefers this dak bangla over all the other places, that's his choice. He is a regular saheb in other ways: he gets angry if his clothes are not ironed properly or his shoes not shined enough or if the driver shows up ten minutes late. But he has his strange ways. For one, he plays the flute. The flute in its wooden case goes with us everywhere, whether we are going to the tehsil office or touring the dhanis or examining road work. I have to carry it myself, like a nursing mother carries her baby, lest someone mishandles it. Whenever he has free time, he takes the flute out and pipes away. Once he has that bit of bamboo in his hands, he is oblivious to all else, doesn't care whether servants are within earshot or dhani folk are milling around. He just plays on, for hours sometimes. This kind of behaviour gives the villagers and servants a chance to get overly familiar. They stand about and listen, speak to him even, telling him they like his playing. The more audacious ones bring their own shepherd's flutes or other instruments and play reedy, shrill tunes until I remind them to stop. Could these good-for-nothing nomads ever look upon a flute-playing Collector with the awe and dignity he deserves, Sir, or be afraid of him in the slightest? Krishan played the flute, and though he is God he was only taken seriously when he preached the Gita, otherwise he was called such names – cowherd, butter-thief and worse. It goes to show that such things barely work in stories, even for gods.

In real life, sahebs must keep the riffraff in their proper place. Sometimes I think it is all this flute-playing and roaming the desert that led to what happened.

No, of course not, I have never spoken about all this to Saheb. I keep my thoughts to myself. At least I, for one, always keep to my place, always observe decorum.

Sure, to go back to our first visit here, it was no different from any of the tours Saheb had taken. The evening we arrived, I unloaded the luggage and Saheb sat reading his files under the naked bulb in the veranda. I unpacked his clothes and books and arranged everything just as he likes – the precious flute-case, magazines and books which came regularly in the mail from Delhi, files and papers. Then I chivvied the staff of the dak bangla into action. As usual, they were all congregated in the kitchen, squatting on the floor, chatting away in some strange dialect, Dhoondhani or Mewati or suchlike. Not one of them was worried that Saheb was tired and hungry, and would soon want his dinner.

The cook began preparing Saheb's meal. In these places, food is never much to speak of – dried beans and berries, spiky, bitter kankoda or sour, ripe-smelling kachari, some yoghurt and gram flour preparation, daal. In Saheb's honour, the staff sometimes procures a chicken or a goat's kid and cooks it with enough chillies to season curries for a whole week. Anyway, Saheb enjoys this kind of food. He likes the thick bajra or jowar rotis, slow-cooked on wood and cowpat fire, buttermilk, palm jaggery – the sort of things people from the headquarters complain about. When dinner was ready, Saheb was still unwilling to come indoors. So we lay the food for him on a bamboo table in the veranda. There was an old paraffin lamp in a corner. Saheb asked for it to be lit and brought to the table as well. He didn't care that it was the surest way of inviting all the insects in the vicinity to dinner too. These kinds of things do not occur to him. As there was no electric fan to keep them at bay, I stood beside him, waving an old straw hand-fan. Saheb ate the food with relish and chatted with that woman, Teejan her name is, who comes twice a day to cook rotis. She brought hot rotis from the kitchen herself, though the two bearers were standing about idly and should have served Saheb instead of chewing tobacco. But she is a bold woman, like all these Banjara women from the desert. You should have seen her looking directly at Saheb and answering his questions about cultivation and grazing even on that first evening. But that wasn't all, there was more to come.

When dinner was over, I brought the English daaru Saheb sometimes drinks. Sure enough, he asked for his flute and, while I made his bed, he played on the veranda. The staff clustered at the kitchen door, straining their ears to hear. Only that woman, brazen like a desert bustard, slunk into the veranda and squatted in a corner. She pulled the rope of the tattered fan, showering Saheb with the sand accumulated in its folds over innumerable desert storms, and listened to the music he made. When Saheb stopped playing, she spoke to him. An illiterate tribal woman addressing Collector Saheb without permission! It is beyond anyone's imagination. But this is what flute music does – people forget themselves and do odd things. She told Saheb how beautiful the melody was, like desert rain and the breeze among bajra stalks and more such nonsense. Saheb smiled and asked the usual questions: How were things in her village? Was the farming all right? She narrated the usual litany: The rains were meagre, there were too many mouths to feed. The Sarpanch was hand in glove with the Naib Tehsildar. And the poor had no saviour. Saheb listened attentively as he always does. After endlessly complaining about the tehsil officials, she added that she wasn't complaining! Soon it would be Saavan, she said. They had been singing to propitiate the rain gods and were hoping for good rains this year – that would solve many problems. Then Saheb asked whether they danced and played music in her tribe. Of course they did! What else do the idlers around here do if not dance and drink and waste time? She, of course, said their dances were beautiful, the most beautiful in the desert, if Saheb saw them he would think whirlwinds were performing for him. She offered to bring some of her tribespeople to perform the next evening under the kalpavriksha.

Yes, she called that evergreen which grows to the north of the dak bangla the wishing tree. You can't miss that tree, it is just a few steps from the veranda. I had noticed it when we had first arrived. It is the only green one among the miserable thorn trees that grow around here. But it is no wishing tree, that is just the kind of nonsense desert folk spout. In truth, it is not even very beautiful, no flowers or fruits, just reddish brown branches and green leaves. It is only made much of here because it seems so lush among the scanty shrub of the desert.

The next day, Saheb went around the villages and dhanis, shaking the Tehsildars and Sarpanches awake, looking through dusty missils and tapaal records. I had packed lunch for Saheb, but he stopped at a poor-looking cluster of huts with a few goats, straggly khejri trees and a couple of raggedy girls going about their chores. He sat on the mud stoop of a hut and spoke to the girls and their mother. The father, an old drunkard by the looks of him, also staggered out and sat staring vacantly. You should have seen how the girls hovered around Saheb, and brought a coarse durrie for him to sit on, a pitcher of water, a worn hookah. They were as bold as you please. You could see plainly that what they could not convey through words, they communicated by their glances. The mother offered Saheb dry jowar rotis and goat's milk, and a chutney redolent with garlic and so red with chillies that just looking at it would make your eyes water. Saheb, of course, ate all of it as if it were the food of gods and complimented the old woman and girls until they were quite giddy. He then gave his lunch – which I had carefully planned and supervised early in the morning and the cook had taken much trouble over – to those hut dwellers. We returned to the dak bangla just as the sun was setting.

The woman, Teejan, brought her tribespeople that evening. In fact, there were so many nomads in the courtyard that it seemed she had brought her entire tribe. By nightfall, there were people squatting in the veranda, talking, coughing, hawking phlegm, tuning their instruments. The two girls from the afternoon arrived too, their braided heads close together, tittering and chattering all the time. After Saheb finished his dinner, he dragged his chair to the edge of the veranda and the performance began. First the women danced in groups, waving their arms, dipping and tilting, moving in a circle. Then a few of them danced with pitchers on their heads, balancing themselves on the raised edges of metal platters. The men played lutes and flutes. Saheb had seen similar things a hundred times over everywhere he went, but he watched rapt as if heavenly maidens were dancing before him. It was almost midnight when the performance ended and Saheb went to bed.

The next two days were spent with the tehsil people and officers who had been summoned by Saheb from the headquarters. He held durbars for the local people, all tribals, some nomadic, some living in dhanis. Such days are busy ones for Saheb and myself. There are too many people and too little time. Saheb works from morning to evening, not pausing for lunch or tea, throwing the entire food-schedule out of kilter.

Yes, those girls came too. They came with their old mother. Thankfully, their drunkard father did not accompany them – he must have been out drinking or sleeping off the taadi from the night before. They waited for their turn to present their petition. Saheb called them over and the Tehsildar too. He chatted with them for some time, looked through the old papers they had brought. Then they left, dipping to the ground before Saheb, grinning broadly, casting sly glances at the tehsil officers. I was standing by the entrance of the room and, as they passed, one of them asked me if I had a long-haired fiancée waiting for me somewhere. I knew then that those girls meant trouble, they were that kind of girls.

The third evening of our stay, the girls brought that old man over – that Sarangiya who plays the bewitched lute. I tell you, that old man is the devil's son-in-law and there is some unholy magic in that sarangi of his. The cook, who is from the mountains in the north, the only one in the staff not from around here, told me that the Sarangiya hung around the dak bangla often. He would come at odd times, not caring whether it was afternoon or midnight, and play that cursed instrument of his. 'I stay out of the old wizard's way and you should stay away from him too,' he said to me when he saw the Sarangiya sitting under the tree. 'The way that sarangi laughs and cries, I am sure there is a human soul trapped in the dead leather and wood.' Of course, the cook now denies saying anything at all, what else could be expected? He is an illiterate servant and is afraid his own shadow will steal his job. However, I heard the sarangi myself and I can confirm that it repeated whatever the old man said like an accursed parrot, answered questions, sang on cue. Saheb was very taken by that old decrepit – dressed like a peacock in his yellow turban, green angrakha and blue dhoti – and by his music. He asked for a wooden seat to be placed for the old man to sit on, and for milk and sweets to be served to him, as if the old nomad were a holy priest.

No, I did not hear all that the old man played. I like a tune or two well enough, but I did not care much for his music. It somehow managed to make everything seem sad and dismal, though God knows there is little to cheer you up around here. He came every night we were at the dak bangla that time and sang, with that devil's instrument repeating whole lines of song after him, joining him in duets. Saheb, too, played his flute for the old man. Can you imagine – the Collector, with his name inscribed on government seals and the entire district bowing before him, playing for an old nomad? That kind of thing unsettles the order, makes you question the entire system. As I said, I don't have a taste for that kind of music, but as they sat outside playing together late at night, it made me uneasy. It was a sound that poured out like water from an earthen pitcher, and just when you think that all the water has drained out, an even cooler, even more silvery stream cascades. Yes, perhaps I am not making much sense. What I mean to say is that the sound lingered and repeated in my head.

The morning we were to leave for the headquarters, I prepared the breakfast tray for Saheb as usual – a cup of tea, well-toasted bread, some butter, and slices of musk melon, the only edible fruit that grows around here. I placed the English newspaper Saheb always reads – and which the driver had driven two hours to fetch – in the tray as well. I took the tray to Saheb's room, but the room was empty. Sometimes Saheb wakes up early and goes for a run, but this morning his running shoes were where I had placed them. I stepped out on to the veranda and saw Saheb almost immediately. He was sitting under that evergreen.

Of course, I was surprised. The garden of our bangla at the headquarters is filled with trees – neem, peepul, mango – but Saheb had never shown any inclination to sit under any of them. Pigeons, sparrows and crows roost on them, and despite the sweeper cleaning the compound twice a day, the ground beneath is invariably strewn with bird droppings. Once, in the cool of the evening, I had laid tea out in the garden, but Saheb just picked up his cup and took it indoors. Of course, there are no bird droppings under this tree. In the open desert around here, only creatures of bad omen, such as vultures and kites, come shrieking, no other birds venture here. Anyway, there was no time to lose that particular morning. We were to leave in an hour for the headquarters. I was already looking forward to an evening at the cinema and other things. I went up to him. 'Breakfast is ready, Saheb,' I said. 'The driver will bring the jeep around in an hour, so we can drive in the cool part of the morning.' When he lifted his head, his eyes were red and he looked tired. I wondered how long he had been sitting there, and whether he had slept at all. Then he rose slowly and walked towards the veranda, turned and looked back once, and entered the bangla. I suppose he was looking at the tree, there's nothing else to look at. The sun was behind the dunes to the east at that time, and its red glow was like roli sprinkled on the tree's glossy leaves. The tree seemed to glow and shimmer. All that nonsense about boon-granting and wish-fulfilling aside, the tree was sort of beautiful that morning, with the sunlight upon it.

Saheb was silent but restless all through the drive back, rolling down the window to half-smoke a cigarette, fiddling with the music player, switching the radio on and off. He wouldn't stop for anything on the way, not even a cup of tea to wet our parched throats. We reached the headquarters around lunch and Saheb went straight to the office without changing or eating. I hurried to the kitchen and got the cook to prepare some sandwiches and sent them to his office. He worked until late, and when he returned his eyes were heavy. Instead of resting, he changed into the clothes he wore for running and went out again.

Yes, he used to go running in the evening at the headquarters. He would thread through the backstreets of the city out to the open desert, and return tired and soaked with sweat.

After that first visit, a few days went by. I did not count how many days, I never do. It is inauspicious – our days are numbered, there's no need to remind the grim Yamraj about that. Anyway, life went on as usual. Saheb worked harder than ever, went running, drank his English daaru, read sometimes. He seemed to sleep very little though. I would hear him play his flute late in the night, early in the morning. Sometimes he played music on the big music machine. That is some machine Saheb has – you can feel the music thumping in your blood, it is that powerful. But he did not hum along with the songs, just sat in silence or walked up and down the room.

One day, Saheb asked me to prepare for a daura again. We were to go back to tour the same tehsil we had visited not many weeks ago. It was a bit unusual. You see, there are plenty of tehsils in Saheb's district, and he generally likes to space out his visits to them. Anyway, it is not for me to say when Saheb should visit a tehsil again, so I kept my mouth shut and packed.

If you ask me, I thought it was those wild Nat girls who, perhaps, were drawing him back. They had come every day while we were in the tehsil, on one pretext or another, and Saheb would always make much of them, admiring their bead-and-silver jewellery, the way they wore their hair in innumerable braids, their colourful scarves. So the following afternoon, we again ate the dry desert dust and reached the dak bangla as evening fell, just like the first time. Saheb jumped out of the jeep as soon as we reached and ran up the steps, not looking right or left. He sat in the living room, flipping through his books, while I arranged his room and filled the buckets with lukewarm water for his bath. After bathing, he went out to the veranda. When I came out to call him for dinner, he was sitting facing north, looking out. He asked for his food to be brought to the veranda, and he was still sitting there when I went to sleep.

No, I couldn't see the veranda from where I slept in the back of the house, in the pantry. But naturally, before going to bed I came to ask Saheb if he needed anything, and that's how I know he was still out in the veranda. In the morning, he was not in his room, but this time I knew where to find him. I carried a folding table and easy chair out to the tree and served his tea there. He ate in silence, leaning back into the chair, his hand stroking the trunk of the tree.

That day, and all through our stay this time around, Saheb did not leave the dak bangla. Instead, people from the tehsil, petty officials and petitioners were all summoned to see him. Saheb got a writing table placed in the sitting room, facing the window towards the north, and worked there from morning to evening. The window framed the tree, some large rocks nearby, and the endless desert burning under the sun like the bloody heat-spawned mirage it is. Saheb always works very hard, not stopping to take a breather, focussing entirely on the problems people bring to him. But it seemed to me as if he was working harder and harder. He ate little and lost weight, there were dark circles under his eyes. He asked the folk at the dak bangla about the old man, that Sarangiya, but they hadn't seen him for a while. Teejan said she would check with the Nat girls, the ones who had brought him round to the dak bangla last time. They were sure to know, she said, they were always running about everywhere.

The next evening, the two sisters came to the dak bangla. They brought some fresh goat's milk and vine-ripened kachari fruit for Saheb, but no Sarangiya. 'He left the day you broke camp,' they said. 'He hasn't been back since. Who knows where he is. The desert is vast and sometimes months go by before we see him.' They spoke boldly and looked at Saheb in a way that made the blood rush to my head. Saheb told them to be sure to bring him over whenever he returned. The girls said there was a man who played the snake-pipes, the magical been which has the power to summon and control snakes. Thankfully, Saheb was not interested in the been player. Later that day, I found a camp cot in the storeroom and a mosquito net, and cleaned them both. I set the cot up under the tree that evening.

No, no one asked me to do so. I was just making sure my Saheb was comfortable. If he wanted to spend the night under the tree, he should at least have some place to rest. If anyone thought what I did was wrong, they never said so. I know Saheb was pleased with the arrangement because he smiled and said something like, 'A camp cot would be a novelty for the princess.' No, I had no idea what he meant. I never try to understand everything he says, it is not my place to do so.

We stayed at the dak bangla for a week that time, and each night Saheb slept outdoors. Yes, I know one of the servants said that he talked to himself, stayed up half the night, smoked ganja – but that servant's a talkative fool with as much restraint as a chattering mynah. In any case, on the eighth morning, Saheb asked me to pack. We were to leave immediately, he had a train to catch the next morning. Yes, it was abrupt, but was it for me to ask him questions? We reached the headquarters around afternoon and Saheb went to the office, remaining there until late. The following morning, he left for Jaipur.

Saheb came back from his leave after ten days or so. I remember the afternoon he returned. It was the day of the rain festival. People here make much of the rain, though God knows it is little and dries up even as it falls. Women, in particular, go crazy. There are swings and songs everywhere, night and day. But there was nothing festive about Saheb when he returned. He looked thinner, paler. He went to the office but did not stay there for long, moved from room to room, smoking and dropping ash. Then he went out, but only as far as the gate of the bungalow. He continued to be restless over the next few days.

One evening, as I was having a cup of tea in the kitchen, he came to the door. He did that sometimes, instead of ringing the bell to summon me. 'You must pack everything,' he said. 'But you have to hurry, we are leaving immediately.' I left my tea unfinished and told the cook to prepare food quickly, there was a daura coming up. Saheb turned back, laughed and said, 'Yes, it is a daura perhaps. Who knows when it will end.' As I said, it is not my job to understand what Saheb means, my job is to carry out his orders. We left before dusk and arrived at the dak bangla by moonrise.

That was over eight months ago. We have been here ever since. We have not gone back to the headquarters even once. Files and ADMs come and go in jeeps from the headquarters, local tribals have become offensively familiar, the Nat girls are around all the time, we eat dry beans and leaves like goats. Soon we will forget everything we have learnt and speak the language of lizards, desert toads and scorpions.

II

STATEMENT OF
THE TEHSILDAR OF ___ TEHSIL

YOU HAVE INCREASED MY honour by calling me here for an interview, Sir. I am a nacheez, a mere nothing, a humble servant of the sarkar. My sole glory is in being appointed the Tehsildar of this tehsil. I have the letter promoting me to the post of Tehsildar framed and hanging in my house. It was signed by the Director Saheb himself. Here, in this tehsil, I am the sarkar's eyes and ears, and arms and legs too, and whatever anyone else says, I always hope to do my duty.

You are both big officers, you and Collector Saheb, your names are in the sarkar's gazette, a long way above mine. What could someone in my humble place tell you about him? But nevertheless, here I am before you, to do my duty as always. I am prepared to answer all questions you put to me. I do see and hear much, being the Tehsildar, but if I am not able to say all that I hear and see, surely you with your wisdom will understand.

No, no, Sir, I don't mean I will hold back anything I know, never. I will always do my duty, always, even if I incur the displeasure of some. And it is my duty to help Collector Saheb. I am willing to do everything to help him. Not that he has ever asked for my help. Why would he? He is the king of the district, he can give orders even to the district officers, so where do I stand? What's my worth, a nothing, a mere Tehsildar like me? My hair has turned grey in this tehsil, and I know every dhoor of the land and the number of babies yet to be born in the dhanis, but what does that count for? I know I am only good for obeying orders. Bring that missil, show records of census, crop yields, household verifications, this and that, bring them soon, bring them now. That's what I hear all the time these days.

Of course, Collector Saheb has every right to give orders. He is a big officer, he can ask for the moon to be put in a child's feeding bowl, but I can only obey to the best of my poor abilties. If I never seem to be able to satisfy him, it's not for want of trying. If there are no records, I can only tell him so. But does he believe me, I who am the sarkari officer of this tehsil? You can be sure he doesn't. He only laughs. 'Bring them,' he says, 'or make an official note in the files that you have lost the records, that you have no idea where they are.' I lost the records? I, who would guard the sarkari records with my life, if need be? I don't eat records, Sir. If some are missing, what can I do? I cannot conjure them – I am not Brahma who created the universe out of a pinch of sand. Some things, only God is aware of. Only He can say where the missing records are, or if they ever existed. Those who want to know, must ask Him and not a mere mortal like me. Besides, some of the records are older than the tehsil office. Even memories are lost with time, Sir, these are mere paper records. Then there are rats and termites, fires and desert storms. Can I control the vermin and the elements, Sir? After all, everything is naashvaan, destructible. So are the records. But Collector Saheb is young, impatient, he wants the seas to be churned in a day. I tell him, first you need to uproot Mandar mountain, then get the snake Vaasuki to agree to be the churning-rope...

No, no, I am not telling you a fable, Sir, just trying to show how things are here, something Collector Saheb hasn't been able to grasp despite every humble effort of mine. Unlike the district and tehsil officers, he is not from around here, he doesn't know the people or the land, and that is part of his problem. Surely you would like to understand the full extent of his issues to be able to help him? He relies too much on the evidence of his own eyes. Eyes see mirages. Does that make them real? He goes on repeating – but I have seen this, I haven't seen that, can't you see this ... For him, khataunis and khasras are everything, and experience and understanding are nothing. I know each hand-width of this land, the crops grown in every chappa, yields, revenues collected and due, defaulters and whiners who come around at collection time, crying and laying their turbans at your feet. I know their drama. You can be sure that their women have kilos of silver jewellery hidden away and their carts have silver sheets nailed underneath. Collector Saheb can trust me to know all this. But does he? No, he'd rather rely on the lying, cheating tribals and the torn bits of records and revenue slips they come clutching in their hands. He'd rather believe their stories of droughts and failed crops, when in actual fact, they have passed the year drunk on taadi, singing and dancing night and day. He believes them when they say they have lived here for generations, when the truth is that they are no better than the vagrant goats they herd, moving around in the desert in search of feed and trying to establish dhanis wherever they find land, completely disregarding whether the land belongs to the sarkar or to another person. They think that, just because they have always lived in it, they have a right over the desert. They tie their camels, build their ugly mud huts wherever they please, and then breed just like the bloody goats they rear. Collector Saheb directly summons Kanungos and Patwaris and even Sarpanches from the villages and listens to them rather than to the tehsil officer ... I have worked here for thirty years, Sir, first as a Patwari and then as a Naib Tehsildar, and I have not seen another Collector like him ... What is the need to change everything that has been established over the years? You can see for yourself the result of all the change and upheaval he has brought about. The magicians and witches of the desert have turned his head.

Who has told me that Collector Saheb has been bewitched? Why would anyone need to tell me? Don't I keep my ears open all the time, and keep one eye open even when I sleep? The people around here are illiterate and most of them are full of nonsense, gibbering about this and that, but they are as cunning as they come. They all know the black magic of this desert. The Thar is a difficult place, Sir, only burning stretches of sand, and yet every child knows where to find water, even their animals know which leaves and berries to eat and which to shun.

The magic is no superstition, Sir, it is real. All of us who live here in the desert have seen the witchcraft of the desert. We know its effect and we have learnt to avoid it. That is the only way to survive. Otherwise, you end up like Collector Saheb, talking to trees and stones, and digging up half the desert in search of a river he has heard about in some story. And the river that he has found and about which everyone's talking from Ajmer to Delhi, it is no river either. It is just a bit of this black magic. How can there be reserves of water under sand? You'll see, it will dry up soon enough, disappear like the desert mirage it is. And do you know, Collector Saheb has been paying compensation to all and sundry for the worthless land he has dug up? He has done it all on his own too, Sir. He has not involved a single tehsil officer. Evaluated the land, determined compensation, identified landholders and made payment directly, just like that, without consulting even me, the Tehsildar. How can I do my duty if he goes on like this?

My apologies, Sir. Yes, of course, I understand that it is for me to answer questions – that's what I am here for – not to ask them.

Yes, Collector Saheb took charge almost three years ago. The previous Collector was from around here. He had come on promotion. He knew the district well. In his time, no Nats or Rabaris would dare cast their eyes upon the Collector, let alone roam in the dak bangla as they pleased. They would wait outside the compound to be summoned. They knew their place and used to bow deeply to all, they'd even say 'ghani khamma' to the orderlies and peons. Now they forget to greet the tehsil officers and, most evenings, there's a swarm of them at the bangla, buzzing like accursed cow-flies.

No, no, the tribesmen were not prohibited from the bangla. The staff at the bangla are all tribals. You can't expect caste-people from proper village settlements to come and live here in the middle of the desert. And there were always performances at the bangla, men sang and played, women twirled around. The previous Collector was fond of the Nat and Kalbelia dances too. But those nomads were kept in their place. They came and went at the pleasure of the sarkari officers. And the performances were accompanied by a feast – laal maans, the best daaru available. A few of us tehsil officers were invited, and we watched the dances in the cool inner rooms. Not like now. Now the dancers dance in the courtyard, and all the dhani folk come carrying tikkads and baatis in cloth bundles, and the whole thing is like a village fair.

Yes, I know the Nat family you speak of. They live in a dhani not far from here. They brought a matter of land records to Collector Saheb's durbar. They had old documents written in some indecipherable script and were making a claim over a patch of khejri trees and the field they cultivate bajra and jowar in. Since they farmed the patch, the khasra had crop and yield records and I, of course, collected revenue from them. It's my duty to collect revenue for the sarkar. Collector Saheb, as usual, got hold of the wrong side of the issue. He said that since there were revenue receipts and the khasra entries went back a long time, that was sufficient evidence that the land had been continuously farmed and occupied by the Nats. I told him there was absolutely no record of their ownership of the land. Do you know what he said in reply? He said, 'But there are always rats, Tehsildar Saheb, and that fire from a few years ago ... You might have lost the records then and, in any case, what are records, just bits of paper.' It was plain he was mimicking me. All those Nats and Kanjars sniggered. I don't mind their laughing at me at all, Sir, for I am a humble man. But they were not laughing at me, they were laughing at the majesty of the sarkar whose servant I am. Even if the Collector doesn't care whether he lowers the dignity of the sarkar, some of us do. He granted a pakka patta then and there. And would you believe me if I told you that the patta was in the name of the woman and not her husband?

Yes, you are right that the man, the father of those two witches, is a good-for-nothing drunkard. Had the patta been in his name, he would most likely have exchanged it for a pitcher of taadi. But still, he is the karta, the head of the family. Assets can never be in the name of womenfolk. Everyone knows women are the most nomadic of nomads, they have no home to call their own. They are born in one family and belong to another, they have no permanence, no roots. They are nobodies without their men. To give the land to women, and Nat women at that ... Everyone wondered about Collector Saheb. 'Doesn't he know that in the Nat tribe prostitution is a profession?' they asked me. 'That the fathers pimp their daughters and turn their homes into brothels?'

No, I don't know whether these Nat women are whores. Perhaps not. Their hut is far from the road, so it can't be easy for clients to reach. Even if they aren't and the Collector, being an outsider, doesn't know about Nats, surely he can see what these women are by the way they look at him sideways, giggling and elbowing each other the whole time. But not him. He can see things in trees and dunes, but can't see that which stares him in the face. I hear that the women come here often, almost every day. They bring food, chat with Collector Saheb, ask him to play the flute. It is scandalous!

Yes, of course I know the old sarangi player. I have been here for thirty years, Sir, there is little I don't know. He has been around for as long as anyone can remember, perhaps even as long as I have been here myself.

No, I don't know which tribe he is from, there are so many of these tribes with lazy menfolk who do nothing but sing and dance like peacocks, in and out of season.

No, I don't know whether he has a permanent home anywhere or where he is now. He is a nomad, he is of no importance. I don't trail after Banjaras who do not pay a paisa in revenue to the sarkar and refuse to play for tehsil functions. He is a rebel and deserves to be flogged. Once, he even turned down playing for the last Collector. 'My music can't be forced,' the old rascal said, as if he were Tansen. If he hadn't left the tehsil the same night, I would have tested that boast in the police station the next day.

When I said he is a rebel, I did not mean he has done anything against the sarkar. He has no land or animals and receives nothing from the sarkar. He is a bit crazy and talks to trees, same as the Collector, but that could be due to ganja.

Collector Saheb? I have heard he smokes ganja, but why ask me? Ask the folk who live in the dak bangla. Ask his orderly, Mathura.

I can't say whether that old Banjara's music is as good as some say it is. As I said, he refused to play at the tehsil office, though he is ready to play anywhere and everywhere, on the roadside or around the bangla here. He is always coming to the dak bangla when he is in the tehsil. This is sarkari property, not for nomads to wander around in, but I have gone easy on him until now, for he is a dokra, an old man with no family to his name. Also, he practises magic like many of these nomads, and I have always tried to steer clear of these wizards. You need to stay away from them, not annoy them or befriend them.

I have never heard him play myself, Sir. My wife, a very foolish woman, had a liking for his music. I remember returning home one evening, many years ago, to find my whole house filled with sweet smells. It wasn't a festival or anything, so I was naturally surprised, and even more so to see the dokra sitting in the inner courtyard, just outside the kitchen. I was naturally angry at his presumption. He had no sense of decorum, venturing right into my home like that while I was away. My wife was in the kitchen, cooking thick rotis coated with real ghee and powdered sugar. Freshly churned chaach stood in a new earthen pot, and a mound of white butter lay in a brass platter. I asked my wife what was going on. 'I am making meethi roti for the Sarangiya,' she said. 'He is there in the aangan.' As if I was a blind idiot. Turned out that he had been playing and singing under the tree on the street corner all afternoon, and my idiot of a wife had been sitting behind the street door, listening to the music and crying her eyes out, instead of drying spices or making papads or doing the hundred other things she could have done in the household. She gibbered about him singing so beautifully, with such sadness, the music wringing tears right out of her heart. She had sent a servant out with alms, but he didn't want any. He wanted to eat meethi roti, the presumptuous glutton, a brazen beggar making demands. So, in return for making her cry, she was cooking rich, sweet bread for him. Though foolish, she was always dutiful and did say she hoped I did not mind. She was pregnant then, so I said nothing, otherwise I might have given her something real to cry about. I am a soft-hearted man, Sir, and within reason, I always make allowances for foolishness in women...

She is not in this world any more, Sir, she is in God's keeping now, which is just as well. She was growing more foolish and forgetful with every passing year. She passed away after giving birth to a fifth daughter, filling my home with five girls, one after another, and not a single son to repay the debt of my ancestors. My younger brother's sons will have to fulfil that duty and give water to the souls of our forefathers, and some day to mine as well – by God's blessings, may that day be far away. Sorry, Sir, this is not related to Collector Saheb and, of course, it could not have been difficult to turn the head of a silly woman like my wife, but this shows he has been practising his arts for long, doesn't it? Though my wife was an ignorant woman and not learned like our Collector Saheb, learning and wisdom are nothing when confronted with the magic of these desert folk.

Of course the dokra knows magic, it is beyond question. Ask anyone in the tehsil and they will tell you. Besides, I have myself seen him use his magic to cure a young woman of her ghost troubles. She was a very beautiful woman, the wife of one of my Patwaris, and the spirits of the desert, always hungry for the likes of her, had claimed her. There were no children or old folk in their home to keep her company and she was always alone. I told the Patwari time and again to send her to my house to visit my orphan girls. She would have been less lonely there with a houseful of motherless girls. But he never did send her. He came from an old Rajput clan and was inordinately proud. I had given him more villages to cover, promoted him in a way, and he had to be out all day. But she would stay inside the patwarghar, never venturing beyond the threshold. I used to be in the vicinity often and never saw her out in the village, except when there was a fair or a festival. One summer, her spirit-affliction increased and she suffered terribly for many days. My Patwari called every vaidya and ojha-guni to treat her. One afternoon, some folk from his village came to the tehsil office and told me she was close to death's door. I went immediately to his house to commiserate and witnessed with my own eyes all that I am going to relate to you now.

When I reached the patwarghar, it was filled with the relatives of my Patwari and his wife. They had travelled from their villages to take a last look at her. There was a lot of wailing and beating of chests. The women, as always, made up foolish death-songs about how she was a young bride, had not enjoyed many rains with her husband, had not given birth to a single child, and now she was being dragged away by greedy spirits. They created much commotion. Meanwhile, one of the village folk mentioned the Sarangiya, and the Patwari himself rushed out to fetch the old magician – he was that besotted with his wife. The Sarangiya came preening and posturing and went straight to the woman. She was lying on a bare string cot, all dishevelled, her face and bosom and legs uncovered. Everyone could see she was suffering terribly in the clutches of the spirits, thrashing and reeling from the poison they had imbued in her. The old magician asked for water to be sprinkled on the mud floor and a cotton mat to be spread. Then he ordered for the woman to be laid on the mat. He squatted beside her on the floor and, taking some potion from his cloth bundle, began rubbing and pressing all of the toes on each of her feet, uttering his magical formulae in a voice like a broken earthen pot. The woman's legs were swollen and the silver paanti and aanti ornaments she wore from her ankles to her shins were biting into her flesh. She was foaming at the mouth. I was certain that she was gone. And yet, that arrogant dokra went on muttering and pressing, pressing and muttering. This must have continued for at least three quarters of an hour, when the silver ornaments began changing colour, turning green with tarnish. Clearly, he was draining the spirit's poison into the silver on her body using his magic. The people crowding around her – even her own clanswomen – moved back. Someone whispered that the shining potion the Sarangiya used was made of mercury. Now everyone knows that silver and mercury are the favourite metals of magicians. Several villagers edged out of the house. When all the silver on her feet turned green, the Sarangiya signalled to the women to loosen and remove the ornaments. Next, he began pressing the fingers of both her hands. Soon the silver bangdis and pahunchis and anants on her arms turned bluish-green too. All her lac choodas cracked from the power of the poison. In the end, he took some wax-like ointment and, placing his thumbs between her brows and his fingers on her temples, pressed. His thumbs and fingers left marks like vermilion tika on the woman's forehead. She immediately stopped writhing and twisting. As the Sarangiya pressed her temples, her face became calm, her eyes closed and she fell into a deep sleep. 'She will be fine when she wakes up. She will never have this trouble again,' he said, as if he knew everything and could see into the future. 'Just don't let her go out in the afternoon in the months of Chait and

Jeth.' And, believe it or not, everything he said was true to the last letter. The woman was completely cured from her spirit-trouble while she lived in this tehsil. Imagine how strong his magic must have been to defeat the powerful desert spirits!

Yes, the Patwari and his family are no longer in this tehsil, Sir. A year or so after the incident, he applied for transfer to another tehsil. I had always helped him, treated him like family. But in the end, he turned out to be an ingrate. He did not consider the favours I had done him and went about bad-mouthing me.

What he said is not relevant, Sir. It was all so long ago and, anyway, he was under the toxic influence of that Sarangiya who visited his home often. Before leaving, he gave five pieces of clothing to that crazy nomad: pagdi, angrakha, dhoti, angocha and jooti. You probably won't know, but the paanch poshak are given only to high-caste priests or gunis. Giving them to the tribeless nomad was scandalous. No one had heard, let alone seen, such wantonness. I am convinced that it was all due to the Sarangiya's magic. You can ask anyone in the tehsil and they will tell you the same.

What more proof do you need? You can see for yourself, the Collector too has lost his senses due to the magic practised by that unholy wizard.

Of course I think he isn't in his senses! How else would you explain what has been going on? Would someone in his senses behave like he does? Would a sane Collector leave his district headquarters and usurp a Tehsildar's tehsil? Would he go about granting land and digging up the desert and consorting with the miserable desert folk? Would he erode the prestige of a Tehsildar appointed by the sarkar, take his authority away and regard him below the lowest of the low Banjaras? If this is not proof enough for you, Sir, I don't know what would be. I just wish that I'd had the good sense to throw that old Sarangiya out of my tehsil years ago, and that Collector Saheb had never set eyes on him. But I know what to do when he comes around next time. I will crush that accursed sarangi and flog every bit of the devil's trickery and magic out of him.

No, no, Sir, I was only trying to help solve Collector Saheb's problem. I will not touch a hair on that old bastard's head if you say so...

Yes, yes, of course. I will bring him round safely to you should he return, for sure I will. I did not mean to do anything wrong, Sir. Perhaps I got carried away somewhat, but I did not mean any harm. I have always done my duty, Sir, and despite being supplanted and dishonoured in my own tehsil, I continue to do so, Sir ... I hope you will note that in your report...

III

THE NAT GIRLS' ACCOUNT

We met Saheb the day he first toured the tehsil, but we had heard that he had arrived at the dak bangla before that. Teejan, who works at the bangla had come around and told us. She was full of praises for him. 'He is handsome like Moomal's lover, like Mahindra,' she said, 'and plays the flute like a second Krishan.' We did not believe her though. The last time she had praised a saheb, he had turned out to be fat and sweaty, and had grabbed at us as we danced.

No, we don't know the name of that saheb, as we don't know the name of this one. What do names matter? A saheb's a saheb. But this time, Teejan turned out to be right, though we think Saheb is more like Dhola of the dreamy eyes, Maru's forgetful husband, than like the warrior Mahindra. We have heard Dhola's story, how he was so beautiful that women forgot to fetch water or light the chulha or rock their babies when he passed by, and how he rode through the desert on the back of his flying camel to bring back Maru. Both Panno and I thought he was Dhola incarnate when we saw him coming across the dunes, only he rode a jeep instead of a camel.

Yes, we know Collectors do not ride camels. You may feel that what we thought of the Saheb has no connection to your question, but you need to know what we thought of him then, what we still think of him. He has been a boon to the whole tehsil, better even than the rains in Ashadh. He is our daata, our saviour. He gave us the patta for our land. We have always lived here, we were born in the dhani and so was our father, yet the tehsil folk would not give a hearing to our claims. The Tehsildar himself said to our mother that the land and the trees belonged to the government. He called everything we told him a story. 'These are all stories. I do not believe your stories,' he'd say. But Saheb listened. He believed us. He said the land was ours and, though Nats, we were settled in our dhani for four generations, so the field we till and our pasture where khejri trees grow belong to us. The khejri trees are precious to us, their leaves are the only food our goats get during the desert summer which lasts almost all year round. They are our boon-givers, our trees of life. And so is Saheb.

No, we didn't say the khejri trees are kalpavrikshas, only that they are like kalpavrikshas. You might see their thorny branches and turn away from their scant shade, but we see their green bounty when all is dry and are grateful for it.

Yes, we had danced with others one night at the dak bangla. The moon was almost full, brighter than a hundred lanterns. Saheb watched from the veranda and liked our dance, and our clothes too! He admired Panno's baajuband and wanted it for his Maru, his beloved!

No, he didn't tell us anything, didn't say that he loved a woman, but why else would he want a bead-armlet? Just as Collectors don't ride camels, they don't wear armlets either.

Saheb had a good time that night, listening to the music, watching our dances. He liked the algoza which the Bhils played, and that made us think of our Sarangiya. He comes around from time to time, like a seller of seasonal wares. We knew he was staying at the big village by the highway at that time. We had seen him there a couple of days earlier. We thought Saheb might be pleased to hear him play his sarangi. His sarangi is magical, it creates an inderjaal, a web of enchantment.

No, Saheb, we don't mean the Sarangiya does jadu-tona, what a notion! It is the pure magic of music which flows from his sarangi, he is well known for it in the desert. When those who have ears of the heart hear it, even if only once, they can never forget it. We have grown up hearing his music. If we close our eyes, we can hear it in the breeze and in the beating of our own blood. But there are also those who think it is just the twanging of strings. The Sarangiya always says he doesn't mind if some people cannot hear the soul of his sarangi. 'My sarangi is not for everyone,' he says. 'It's not given to everyone to feel and understand beauty.' A few years ago some rich folk from a big city by the sea had heard him play in the marketplace and wanted to capture his music in their machines. They promised much money, much fame, but the Sarangiya wouldn't agree. Everyone tried to convince him. 'The seths will make sure you feast on milk-sweets and have English daaru to drink every day,' they said to him. But he wouldn't hear of it. 'You cannot hold a river in your cupped hands,' he replied. 'You cannot imprison the soul of my sarangi in a machine.' He left the area quietly one night and did not return for a long time afterwards.

We only know about the Sarangiya's music, we don't know much else about him. We don't even know his name. Everyone just calls him the Sarangiya around here. He is the player of the sarangi, that's all there is to know about him, that's all that matters. We don't know where he comes from or where he goes. One day he is here, sitting under the fine shade of a babool tree, smoking his chillum at dusk as the sky turns the colour of dust raised by cattle-hooves, and the next day he is gone. He says he has taken a vow to play music to a different sand dune every night, and once he runs through the dhors around here, he moves on.

What a question! Of course, he is only joking. Why would he play to the barren dhors? He can't fill his belly with sand and sunrays any more than you can. He plays for food and money and bottles of Kesar Kasturi, just like the other kalavants here. You mustn't believe the idle talk about Thar magic, Saheb. There is no magic in the desert, only hunger and hardship.

Yes, we went to the big village the next day. We were planning to go to the marketplace in any case, we had things to sell: kachari, sangari, leaf baskets.

What else is there to sell? We sell these things, things which are of the desert. You can see for yourself, the sand does not yield a bounty. We sell what we can.

Yes, of course we have grown in the desert too, but what has that to do with the things we trade? We are nothing special, we are common like the dhors and the bawaliya plants here, but we are not to be traded.

Yes, the Sarangiya was at the haat. When we had sold all our wares, we went to him and told him about Saheb.

We don't make up stories, we told him exactly what we told you, what we had learnt about the Saheb in those early days of his coming here: that he is like the hero of our songs, tall and beautiful, with eyes the colour of honey, and that he is a kalavant himself and also very generous. The Sarangiya laughed at that. 'A generous artist,' he said. 'Generous with his art or his purse?' He is always joking like that, the Sarangiya. But if you look closely, you can see his eyes are sad, he has a heartache. How else can his sarangi make such music, unless its strings are bathed in tears, in the heart's blood?

He accompanied us to the dak bangla that evening. Saheb was on the veranda when we reached, and called to us to come in when he saw us. The Sarangiya can be prickly sometimes, but he saw straightaway that Saheb could hear with his heart. We stayed there for some time while he played for Saheb. He played on and on, one song after another. Finally, we left when the moon had come up an arm's length in the sky, and he was still playing and Saheb was still listening, his eyes fixed on the Sarangiya.

Yes, the Sarangiya told stories too, or rather story-songs. We have heard some of them. He has the usual repertoire of love stories that every tune player knows – Dhola–Maru, Padmavati–Ratan Singh, Jasma Odhan. And then there are some we have never heard except from him, like the one about a prince who assumed the form of a goat for the love of a village girl, or the reed princess who lived by a pond and fell in love with a shepherd-boy. How can we say whether any of these love stories are true? But it is certain that, under the desert sun, only the hardiest things grow – like us Nats and black deer and khejri and keekar – so why not persistent, maddening love which cares nothing for life or sanity? It is a part of the desert's hardships.

We haven't seen the Sarangiya for a while now, since the end of the month of Jeth, in fact. We thought he might return after Bhadon, but he hasn't. There's nothing surprising about that though. He has no home or wife or camel to call his own.

One day he is here plying his bow on the sarangi like we ply our needles over our kanchalis, and the next day he is out following a desert trail.

We don't know of anything that might help you find out what's wrong with Saheb, as you put it. Actually, we don't think there is anything wrong with him at all. He is all right, it is the world which is wrong for him. He ought to have lived only in a story.

IV

THE GUARD'S STORY

My name is Kanamal Bhil, Hukum, and I have worked at this dak bangla for a long time. I don't know how old I am or how long I have been here, but when I first arrived, I still had the taste of my mother's milk in my mouth and played with my glass kancha beads. My father's hair and moustaches were still dark and fragrant like the desert deer. My father's been dead two score years and, at the time of his death, his hair was grey like a winter evening and his moustaches drooped like the arches of a fallen fort. Now you can estimate for yourself how long I have been here.

No, I haven't always been the guard for this dak bangla. My first job was that of a helper to the man who looked after the camels the firangi sarkar kept here. The camels were used to fetch supplies from the villages, and memsahebs used to take joyrides on them sometimes. He was stern, the camel-man, and came from another desert, the one across the mountains north from here. He sometimes told stories of the large herds of sheep and camel his tribe kept, of cold pastures in the mountains, wool carpets their women wove and the meats they feasted on. As I speak with you, I can see him clearly – leaning against a leather saddle in the stable behind the main building, pulling at his strange hookah, and pausing to scold me for spilling the camel-feed, though neither the stable, nor he, nor indeed the camels, are here any more.

This, of course, is much before the Sarangiya came. The camels were gone and the gora sahebs too, by the time he arrived. To me, though, everything that has happened in the past is fresh, as if it has just happened. Each day, as my age increases, my memory burnishes, grows brighter like silver coins polished with use. I can't explain why this is so. I know that the older you grow, the less you are supposed to remember. Age gives you maan – the honour to be remembered and the right to forget. At times, I think I myself am a memory from the past ... I am the only one left who knows the past now, the only one who can tell old stories and, with each telling, I remember them better. Usually, I tell them to myself, for who else is there to hear them?

No, while my name means a one-eyed man, there is nothing wrong with my eyes. You can say, though, that they are older than the rest of me. My mother used to say my eyes were formed before the rest of me in her womb. She used to dream of two large eyes floating deep inside her, and the dream disturbed her. When I was little, she used to fret about how fixedly I gazed at everything around me. 'This boy never blinks,' she used to say to my grandmother. 'It was the same when he was in my womb, Mai, he sees too much. How will he go through life seeing like this? He is sure to have an evil wish cast upon his eyes.' In order to calm her fears and protect my gift of sight, my grandmother named me Kanamal, the one-eyed. And it has served its purpose, I can tell you, Hukum. I can see better than the young folk around here. The only one who sees better than me is Collector Saheb. All the others are purblind. Take the young orderly, for example. Despite the gift of two clear eyes, he is blind to the beauty and invitation of the desert spring all around him. He continues to brood on the sights and pleasures of the city – and such poor pleasures that the memories of them make him miserable.

Why should memories of past pleasures make us unhappy, Hukum? The real pleasures are those whose memories give ineffable joy, like the joy on the face of a sleeping child sated with milk. The true joy of suckling at his mother's breast is part of him and saturates him. There are few true pleasures, and even fewer are those who are able to recognize them. The orderly is unfortunate because he can't see his good fortune. What could be better than to be here now, when Collector Saheb has revived the desert spring?

No, I don't mean just the river. The river is a part of it, but the desert spring is everywhere – the trees, the dunes, the desert breeze are all filled with its beauty. If you close your eyes, you see it better. If you look inside, you see it everywhere.

Riddles? How else could I speak about a mystery except in a riddle? I have not solved the riddle, I don't want to, there is no need to solve it, for the riddle itself is a true pleasure.

I am answering your question about Collector Saheb. This is the answer – Collector Saheb is experiencing a true pleasure, a once-in-a-thousand-lifetimes pleasure. He has given himself to beauty and now he can see it everywhere.

As you wish, Hukum, I will try to answer the way you want me to, not tell stories as you say. But if answers are in stories, what can I do?

The tree? That tree? It was here when I arrived, tall and leaf-laden, the shade of its beauty fell everywhere. From my first day here, I noticed its beauty. 'How can a tree be this beautiful?' I asked my boss, the camel-man. He stared at me. 'It's an ordinary tree,' he said. 'Don't be stupid.' But I wasn't stupid. Can an ordinary tree have a trunk as smooth and glowing as a copper surahi? Can its leaves dazzle like emeralds? The camels were wiser than that camel-man – they always respectfully circled the tree on their way in and out of the stable, and never stretched their arched necks to taste its leaves. No one touched the tree, neither bird nor beast. Only Hiraman parrots sometimes perched on it, and the full moon. I bow to it, dawn and dusk, before the sun rises and after the lamps are lit, for its beauty does not need the light of either to glow. I don't think everyone sees the real beauty of the tree, but if they don't, am I, Kanamal, responsible for their blindness or for my own ability to see?

I have known the Sarangiya for long. He has been coming to this part of the desert before the road which leads from the city to the dak bangla was built. At that time, sahebs visited only during the short winter months. The Sarangiya used to come often, I think oftener than he does now. He does not need roads to travel, the desert is full of paths, but it seems that none of them lead to the place he is trying to reach ... Then, as now, he used to come to the dak bangla, sit under the tree or by the large rock you can see at some distance, and play his sarangi. Sometimes, especially on full moon nights, he played until the moon set. When morning came around, his arms would be as stiff as the wood of the sarangi and his eyes would be like sun-mirrors. His sarangi has learnt to speak due to his penance. It has learnt to cry. Not everyone knows how to cry. The Sarangiya himself doesn't know how to – he is too proud. His eyes burn but not a drop falls. That instrument of his has to do all the crying for him.

You wish to know, yet complain when I try to tell you. Everything I say sounds like a riddle to you.

Tehsildar Saheb says the Sarangiya practises magic? Who is to say why the Tehsildar says what he says? Tomorrow he might say that sunrays can be reaped like ears of maize. Would you ask me to give reasons for that too? The fact is that he too can see very little. He is one of the tribe of the purblind. He can only recognize beauty that he can crush. When he is faced with the Sarangiya's music, confronted by the kind of beauty that defies pollution, that has been distilled through sadhana and is ever-fresh, he can't understand it and thinks it is magic. There are many of these things that the Tehsildar does not understand. No, there is no magic in the Sarangiya or his sarangi. It is art that he possesses, he is a guni, one with knowledge and skill. To explain the Sarangiya's art as magic is not right. It takes away from the penance he has done to acquire it.

You want to know why the Tehsildar speaks ill of the Sarangiya, Hukum? Is that, too, a riddle for you? He is a fearful man, the Tehsildar. You see him blustering and shouting, but look closely and you can see all his fears. He himself never looks closely, never searches – he is even fearful of seeing his fears. Perhaps that is the reason he dislikes the Sarangiya, who is not afraid, who is always on a quest.

No, Hukum, this is not a riddle at all. Let me tell you about an incident involving the Tehsildar and the Sarangiya from a few years ago and you will understand. This is before the time of the present Collector Saheb. A big saheb was camping at the dak bangla and the Tehsildar used to come to visit him sometimes. The big saheb had heard about the Sarangiya from city folk who had come for the famous camel fair. 'You are the Collector of the district and you have not heard him play?' they asked. 'There's no music like his. Hear him once and you will forget everything else.'

So the Tehsildar was summoned and ordered to find the Sarangiya. It was the middle of Ashadh and the Sarangiya happened to be in the area. The Tehsildar sent me to fetch him. 'Tell him he has to perform at the dak bangla this evening,' he commanded. I carried his orders to the Sarangiya. 'Am I a trained monkey or performing bear?' he asked. 'Your Tehsildar thinks he just has to ask and the sun will bow before the moon. But I will come. There is a waxing moon tonight. I will play under the tree, I will try to invoke her.' I was not surprised. If he was around, the Sarangiya usually wound up at the bangla with the moon.

He arrived that evening at dusk. The big saheb was taking his bath and the Tehsildar was standing on the veranda, waiting impatiently. He bowed briefly to the Tehsildar. 'I am willing to perform,' he said, 'but I will play under that tree, for I can only play in the open, my music does not flourish in closed rooms.' Tehsildar Saheb swelled with anger. 'Stop this nonsense, you old scoundrel!' he shouted. 'You will make conditions with the sarkar? If the big room is good enough for others to dance and sing in, it is good enough for your old been.' The Sarangiya raised his eyes and looked at the furious Tehsildar. Quietly, he turned and walked towards the gate. The Tehsildar shouted angrily after him, 'Don't let me hear you twang your instrument here. I will break it into pieces smaller than grains of sand, you charlatan!'

The Sarangiya passed me at the gate. His face was like a hail-filled cloud. 'That ignoramus does not know the difference between a sarangi and a been,' he hissed as he exited the compound. 'Why should I play for him and that other man, who know about music less than an owl knows about sunlight? I am a kalavant, my art is for my own pleasure. I am not a bhaand who sings for money.' He looked up to where the sky was silvering. 'It is panchami today, the fifth night of the waxing moon,' he muttered to himself. 'The moon is slender and glowing like you, but I won't be able to play to you.' He didn't go far though, just to the big rock there. As the moon rose, brightening the sky and deepening the shadows on the earth, he began playing. The breeze carried the music everywhere, to the tree in the courtyard and to the Tehsildar inside the bangla. One of the bearers came running out. 'Do something, make that madman stop!' he said. 'The Sahebs are crackling furiously, like a babool tree on fire!' What could I do? I couldn't chase the desert-dweller out of the desert any more than I could stop the breeze, or throw a stone and knock the moon out of the sky. So I did nothing and stood still.

Later that night, the Tehsildar came out of the bangla, full of daaru and anger. He used to ride a motorcycle then, the kind that makes a lot of noise. Phut, phut, phut, it would go and startle everyone. He used to leave it a short distance from the bangla. Walking towards it, he shouted at me for allowing beggars to play around the bangla. 'I will dock your pay and get the constable to round up the beggars tomorrow.' He turned to cast an angry look in the direction of the great rock where the Sarangiya was still playing. Suddenly, he froze. 'What is that, what is that?' he cried. His voice shook, his hair stood on end.

I looked in the direction of the rock too. The moon, though new and threadlike, was casting a bright light, and I clearly saw the Sarangiya perched atop the rock, the sarangi resting against his shoulder, his head swaying in enjoyment of his own music. 'That is the old kalavant, Hukum. The Sarangiya,' I said.

But the Tehsildar was past comprehending. He was moaning and clutching at his hair like someone demented. His body shook as if he had contracted the fevers of Magh. Then, he pitched forward and fell as if someone had cut the legs from under him. I tried to help him and called to the bearers in the bangla. 'Oh, the horror, the horror,' he kept repeating. We couldn't raise him. He shrank from our touch as one shrinks from hot coal. We did not know what to do. The big Saheb had drunk a lot of daaru and had fallen asleep, and Doctor Saheb was a two-hour jeep ride away. I asked the bearer to call the Sarangiya. Perhaps if the Tehsildar saw him, he would realize it was just the musician, no more to be feared than his own shadow. The Sarangiya came willingly enough, and stood before the Tehsildar whose teeth chattered in his head. He was shaking so violently, we thought his soul would detach from its moorings and float away. He made violent efforts to close his staring eyes. We were all confused. 'What is it? Can't he see it's you? What is he seeing?' The Sarangiya smiled and turned his shining, mirror-eyes at me. 'I can't say what he sees,' he said, 'a snake or a demon or a crying woman. But he certainly does not see me. Take him inside, he will do harm to himself. See, he is clawing at his eyes.' In truth, the Tehsildar had scratched his face. He was a terrifying sight. 'Tie his hands and sit with him tonight,' the Sarangiya said. 'I won't play any more. He has stained the night with ugliness.'

We fetched a bedsheet, swaddled the Tehsildar like a baby and carried him inside. The bearers sat with him and, the next day, the driver brought Doctor Saheb from the city. The Tehsildar was sick for many days, delirious with fever. Slowly, he began recovering. His family held a puja and invited priests and mendicants alike to eat his bread and bless him. I went too. I wanted to wish him well. When the feast was over, the Tehsildar called for me. Even before I could say 'ghani khamma' and ask after his well-being, he asked about the Sarangiya. 'Where is he? Is he still around? Have you seen him? Has he asked about me?' I told him the Sarangiya had left at the beginning of Saavan. He seemed relieved. He has avoided the Sarangiya ever since, has not asked him to play or tried to stop him from coming to the dak bangla again. He does not even mention him.

What did the Tehsildar see? I can't say, Hukum. I never asked him. Perhaps nothing, perhaps everything. But I do believe that it wasn't the Sarangiya who inspired his terror. It was he himself. The fearful sight which he could not bear without losing all reason, it came from himself.

I am telling you – I, Kanamal Bhil, who sees better than most – the Sarangiya was just the same that night, the same beauty and pain coursed around him as it always does. There was nothing to fear. Sometimes people see better when they first see their own weakness, and sometimes they shut their eyes tighter, grasp everything harder. You have talked to the Tehsildar. So this is a riddle you can answer yourself.

The Sarangiya? What about him? Some things he sees, towards others he too is stone-blind. He wants to know the sun by fixing his eyes on it and then complains that all is dark. That is his way. Now our Collector Saheb understands that to know the sun, you must give up the quest for light and become shade first. For who knows the sun better than his wife, chaaya, who exists because of the sun and yet can hold him back?

Perhaps you are right, perhaps what I say doesn't make any sense. After all, as the young orderly says, the desert sun has been baking my brains all these years. But whether I make sense or not, I know that Collector Saheb has a gift of sight that transcends mine. You only have to look at him to know he sees the fine layers in shadow and sunlight, just as he saw the hidden river and the covert injustices meted out to the dhani folk here.

Yes, he sleeps under that tree. I don't know whether he talks to the tree or the tree whispers to him. All is enveloped in the sapphire blue shade the tree casts nightly. That tree is like the desert – it creates visions and mirages. And only those who can bear its beauty are able to tell the difference between the two.

Why would you wish to know, Hukum? Collector Saheb has experienced something you can't. He does not want to prove it to anybody, he is content in his ecstasy. He has revived the lost desert spring. Everyone seems satisfied, no one sees a need to pry. Except the Tehsildar. And now you.

No, Hukum, I don't smoke ganja. I have never seen Collector Saheb smoking it either. He works and plays his flute. I don't know where the Sarangiya's village is. He mentioned spending the rainy season with a tribe of Rabaris, the ones who keep camels. He said he travels with them sometimes. He might have gone to the cattle fair with them – it happens about this time. I can't say for sure. He is a kalavant, an artist, free like the desert breeze which abides by its own almanac. When the time is right, he will return.

I am sorry, Hukum, if you don't think you are any further along in your investigation than you were before speaking with me. Perhaps that is so – the truth does not always take you forward, but it can help you see.

V

ACCOUNT OF A CAMEL-HERDER (AS REPORTED BY THE CONTROLLER OF THE CAMEL FAIR AT ___)

I OWN A FLOCK OF camels, Bikaneri and Mewati, the best of their kind. Some I have inherited from my father and some I have bred myself. I can tell you the month and year when each of them was born, the rains that year, the crop, the price of maize. When you see them walking across the dunes with their swaying, wave-like gait which even the divine dancers of Inder's court envy, your eyes are cooled by their beauty. There is nothing more enchanting than a train of camels, golden like the sun, trailing across the desert, leaving shallow footprints on the soft sand in which toads and lizards find shelter. I go with my camels everywhere, sometimes leading, sometimes following them. I have been as far west as Jaisalmer and up to the oasis in the north, and once I took my camels to a big school in Bikaner where boys and girls from the city learn about camels from books and from us camel-herders.

I know the desert. I have crossed and recrossed it for two score and ten years. But what I know about the desert is like a mote of sand when compared to the Sarangiya's knowledge. He knows the trails and waterholes, places forbidden to venture in by ancient travellers, and the thaans of desert gods. He can always find the right place to camp so that the vagrant night-wind of the desert does not turn the camels into mounds of sand. And what he does not know about herbs and berries for food and medicine, and cures for illnesses of camels and humans alike, is not worth knowing. Truly, he knows the desert and its lore like I do the names and ages of my camels. The Sarangiya is the only one who is not of our tribe and yet is allowed to touch our sacred phad, on which stories of the valour of Pabu-ji, our warrior god, are painted. In his memory are more song-stories of Pabu-ji than our priest, the old Bhopa-ji himself, who has been singing Pabu-ji's songs for as long as my own old father remembers. The Sarangiya does not need the aid of the roll of cloth either, for the songs he knows are not to be found illustrated on the fifteen-foot phad. Nor are they painted on the old sixty-foot one which our ancestors used for worship. All he needs is his sarangi. The sarangi is his companion, his sweet-throated, obedient wife who accompanies him word for word.

Yes, he knows magic, the golden magic of the desert. We all know that magic, all of us to whom the desert belongs.

We have been learning it for a long time, from the sun and the barren sands, smoothly golden and burning day after day after day, ever since the god Shiv put us down here in the Thar to tend to the divine camels of Parvati, his wilful wife. That magic protects us, and the scorching sand we eat every day, the fires of the desert we walk through, all nourish us instead of burning us to cinders. If you don't believe it, come and live here for a few summers. The Sarangiya sings a song in which the true lover is turned into deep, dark shade by the scorching sun, and the false one is blown away like sand by the winds.

Whether I know the Sarangiya or not, who can say? But I have spent many months travelling with him in the desert since I was a youth. For many years, we have played together – I, my ravanhatha and he, his sarangi – at Bhaumiya-ji's thaan where snakebites and other poisons are cured, and have shared a campfire and tikkads at the camel fair. He used to like the music I made with the ravanhatha. It is nowhere close to the elaborate sarangi he plays, being a mere single-string instrument of goatherds and Rabaris. But like the sarangi, it too is made of wood and goat hide, it too is played with a bow. And it is older than the sarangi in this desert. Sambal, Shiv's man, made it and played it while grazing his camels. I used to say to the Sarangiya in jest, 'My ravanhatha is the older brother of your sarangi, so you ought to treat me with favour, like a doting husband treats a favourite brother-in-law.' And he did – he treated me with such favour that I will remain indebted to him in all my subsequent lives.

The year the Sarangiya and I went travelling together for the first time was a dry year in my village. The rains had not arrived, though the whole of Ashadh had passed. Even elder folks had not seen such a dry spell. 'There are no tears left in Mata Devi's eyes,' they said and herded the whole village to the shrine of the goddess. We prayed night after night, but the rains still did not come.

One morning, I decided to shear designs into the flanks and backs of my camels, to lighten their hair so that they suffered less in the heat. There was little fodder left for them, but what could I do? The trees around our village had no leaves left. It broke my heart to see their patient, sad eyes, their skin hanging in folds where the flesh had melted away. I had finished the shearing and was plucking a tune on my ravanhatha when the Sarangiya passed by. He had his cloth bundle on his head and the sarangi across his back. He stopped as he always did at the sound of my lute and laid down his bundle.

'Music in the desert is like a magnet,' he had said once. 'Even the hoarse toads and mute scorpions will come to hear if you know how to play a song.' When I finished my song, he picked up his bundle again. 'I am leaving,' he said, 'I must journey on.' Then he patted one of my young calves. 'Your camels need food,' he said. 'There's been rain some fifty kos west from here.'

'Are you going in that direction?' I asked.

'I am. I want to see the raindrops falling like rows of pearls from the sky's odhani.'

'Then I shall come with you.'

I quickly wrapped some jowar rotis in a piece of cloth, filled as many hollow gourds as I could find with water, and collected the few bundles of dry leaves that remained for my camels. I loaded the Sarangiya's small bundle on the back of a calf and tugged at the rope passed through the nostrils of my lead camel. He rose gracefully, first to his knees and then on to his long legs. I pointed him westward. The rest of the flock followed and we set out.

We journeyed during the mornings and early afternoons, sheltered by the moving shadows of my camels. When the sun burned right above our heads, we dug hollows under the dunes and rested, resuming our march in the cool of the evening and travelling on until night darkened. When we were tired, we made camp in the open desert. I called the lead camel to a halt and the whole train came to rest in a semicircle, their humps towards the wind, necks laid low along their sides. I fed them the dried leaves and talked to them, told them that the rains were not far away, that soon they would have sweet rainwater and fresh, green fodder.

We ate the jowar rotis, smoked the Sarangiya's chillum and played our instruments.

At the beginning of our march, the Sarangiya led the camels, but a few days into the journey, the camels sensed the rain too. They knew the direction they must take and became excited and eager. The young calves in the train ran out of line and needed to be called back again and again. Even my experienced lead camel became frisky out of season, nudging and worrying the females. This slowed us down, but we are at home everywhere in the desert, so neither the Sarangiya nor I minded. The Sarangiya used the diversions to collect dry berries and desert herbs, and when the jowar rotis I had brought ran out, he mixed the herbs into the dry flour he had in his cloth bundle and made thick, crusty tikkads. We cooked them on cloth bundle fire and ate them dipped in camel milk – a feast fit for kings.

One night, when we were a few kos from the rains, our sleep was broken by the cries of one of my calves. He stood stamping his long, slender legs, letting out cries of pain that made my heart crumble like a rock of salt. I sprang up and ran towards him. The moon was big and bright, and in the silver light I saw a black shadow clinging to the flank of my calf. It was a snake, coiled like a nagali earring and hanging with its poisoned fangs on to my poor, frightened calf. Maddened with fear and pain, he was shivering and wailing. I began to cry too, I couldn't bear his suffering. I am a Rabari, the camels are my children, and my soul hurt at my calf's pain. Everyone knows that snakebites in the open desert are fatal – the cold and heat alike act to enhance the poison. I had no hope of saving his life and was watching helplessly when the Sarangiya shook me by the shoulder. I had not noticed him coming up to me.

'Make the calf kneel. Do it quickly,' he said.

I pulled at the dragging rope, and the calf collapsed. The Sarangiya deftly pulled the snake off him and threw it into the hollow where our cooking fire still smouldered. He threw some dry camel dung on it and it flared. The snake writhed and shrivelled in the flames. I held the long, beautiful head of my camel in my arms. His cries rent my heart. The females in the train were milling around, trying to get close. The calf was trembling violently, his body going into spasms.

'Do something,' I cried to Sarangiya. 'Save him!'

He looked at me for a moment. 'It is difficult, very difficult, but I will try,' he said.

He untied the thread he wore around his neck – a thick red, yellow and black thread from which hung a silver tablet – and tied it around the calf's leg, just above the hock. Next, he drew out a sua needle from his turban, heated it in the fire and branded the bite-wound. Then he took a pinch of ash from the fire and began rubbing it into the wound, chanting prayers under his breath. He repeated this again and again, praying and rubbing the warm ash in and around the wound, until the moon set and the sky separated from the desert for the day.

The sun rose and, like a second miracle, so did my calf, shaky and trembling. There is no more beautiful sight than a sick camel rising to his legs. Once he is up, the danger has passed. The Sarangiya looked pale like the setting moon, though. He sat on his haunches, holding his sarangi in both hands, as I got the train together for the day's march. The rains were close at hand now and the flock stepped out eagerly but, as the day wore on, the Sarangiya got slower and slower. I urged him to ride on one of the camels. When we stopped to rest in the afternoon, instead of sitting propped up against a rock and playing scraps of song on his sarangi as was his wont, he laid himself down in the sand, wrapping himself in his sheet. He could not eat the tikkads I'd cooked, and by evening he had sunk into a stupor. His wide open eyes stared sightlessly, his mouth was sealed into a line. I placed him on the back of the lead camel and hurried my flock on.

The camels made straight towards the rains and, by midnight, we were close to a large village. There was a baoli at its outskirts, filled to the brim with sweet water – rainwater, not the briny water which comes from deep within the old earth. I lowered the Sarangiya on to the steps of the baoli and propped his head up on a cloth saddle. Then I soaked my shoulder-cloth in cold water and wiped his face, moistened his lips, filled the hollow gourds and dripped water on to his feet, his hands. All night, he lay motionless, not a word nor sigh came from him.

In the morning, folk from the village came to fetch water and were surprised to see us. I told them about the snake and how the Sarangiya saved my calf, absorbing the snake's poison himself.

'We have Bhaumiya-ji's thaan here,' the villagers consoled me. 'He will cure your friend.'

They carried him to the chaupal in the centre of their village. The women came to see him and wept out of pity and reverence. Later in the evening, the old people of the village arranged prayers for Bhaumiya-ji. I played my ravanhatha and the men chanted hymns in praise of the great subduer of snakes. The women, too, gathered and sang songs of protection late into the night.

Everything came to a standstill in the village as we prayed to Bhaumiya-ji for seven days and six nights. Even the rains held back. Though clouds gathered every day, only a few drops actually fell. The Sarangiya remained unconscious the whole time, his unseeing eyes open, his breath so soft that the thread the village vaidya held before his nostrils to check his breathing barely moved. On the seventh day, the rains finally fell in abundance and the air hummed with its music. I brought the sarangi and laid it close to the Sarangiya.

'She has been silent for so many days,' I said to him. 'You must make her sing with the rain for Bhaumiya-ji. His shrine here is famous.'

The priest at the shrine had consecrated a thread for his protection. I tied it around his arm, but there was no flicker of consciousness in the Sarangiya, as if he too was made of wood and leather. Nothing seemed to be able to quicken the life in him.

The rain stopped towards the evening and the scent of wet earth filled the air. I sat on the steps of the chaupal. A waning moon, white like a piece of limestone, rose in the sky. Crickets chirruped like silver anklets and the peacocks called to the shy peahens. In the light of the earthen lamps burning on the chaupal's steps, I saw a shimmering cloud of tiny insects rise from the earth, their translucent wings and incandescent bodies undulating in a rainbow-like arc towards the raindrop-festooned branches of the khejri and babool trees. Like a string of jewels, they glowed and glittered. As I watched them, I heard a sound from the corner where the Sarangiya lay, and turned.

The Sarangiya, who hadn't moved since I took him down from the back of my camel, was sitting upright on his pallet. 'Princess,' he cried. 'Princess.' The rest of his words were incoherent. I wept. This was the final delirium, I thought. I called out loudly and the folk from the village came running.

I supported the Sarangiya in my arms and asked for holy water to moisten his mouth. 'Any water will do, I am thirsty,' he whispered hoarsely. In the light of the moon, we saw that his open eyes were no longer unseeing. He smiled at me and whispered, 'I saw her...' The crisis was over.

A little while later, he drank a bowl of warm goat's milk and fell asleep. He slept soundly that whole night and the next day too. All the time that I tended to him as he recovered, my heart was filled with gratitude. I prepared corn and buttermilk gruel for him and played his favourite tune on my lute every day. As he grew stronger, he picked up his sarangi again and, before we left the village, we played at Bhaumiya-ji's thaan to thank him.

During our onward journey, the Sarangiya told me about himself for the first time, about the little village he was born in, somewhere further west, and how he came to hear of the Princess.

'It was a tough life in our village,' he said. 'Everyone worked, every little man-child. The men farmed, women did odd-jobs, gathered cowpats and firewood, and fetched water, children tended to goats and camels. My father, though, was different. He was a true artist. He played all the instruments of this desert, told stories, sang and danced. When he tied little brass bells around his ankles, picked up his kartal or sarangi and performed, his whole being glowed with joy.

There might not have been food in his belly, but there was always a song on his lips. He was always ready to perform for friends and villagers and visitors.

'But there was me and my brothers and sisters who needed to be fed, and the small jowar field on the outskirts of the village that needed to be tilled – so my mother complained when my father tuned his sarangi. "There is work to be done, the field to be weeded and fodder to be cut, and you are playing music like you are granted strings of gold coins from the king's court every quarter," she would say. "Wait until a king hears my music, my songs, then I will cover you in ornaments of gold, from the borla on your head to the beechee on your toes. You will shimmer and glow and tinkle, and your aad necklace will reach below your navel," my father would answer. But he played less and less. The vital, glowing happiness which animated him and mesmerized me, manifested less and less. His instruments gathered dust and the brass bells became tarnished, their strings frayed.'

The Sarangiya's family kept goats for milk and meat. Young goats are more difficult to rear than the young of any other animal – the kids succumb to both excessive heat and cold, falling like dry leaves on summer days and winter nights. But once they mature, they need little care. They can practically look after themselves and can be tended to even by children. So when the Sarangiya turned six or seven, his mother set him to work looking after their flock of goats.

She would give him thick rotis and a bit of onion or a lump of jaggery, and send him out after the goats. The Sarangiya would tuck in his waist a bamboo-and-string toy sarangi his father had bought him at a fair, pluck a stick from a keekar tree, and spend the day playing the instrument while the goats grazed.

Once, the goats wandered close to the field where his father was at work. The Sarangiya perched on a bit of rock and played away on his toy, filling the air with shivering notes, as children do. But even then, there was something ethereal in the music he made with the shrill toy. His father left the bullocks standing in the field and came up to him.

'Who taught you to play like that, Chhora,' he asked the Sarangiya.

'You did,' he replied. 'I learnt from hearing you and watching you and trying every day.'

His father stood silent for a while, looking fixedly at him, then went back to the waiting bullocks.

'I could not understand my father's expression,' the Sarangiya told me. 'I was afraid he was angry with me, so I slunk home quietly that evening. I found my father sitting at the threshold of our hut, smoking his coconut hookah. "Come here, Chhora," he said. "Bring the algoza. We will begin our lessons with the simplest instrument first." From that day onwards, he taught me how to play his instruments despite my mother's grumbling. "The boy works during the day and so do I," my father said to her when she complained more than usual. "He only learns in the evening. Let me teach him."

'Over the years, he taught me everything he knew, and told me the stories he had turned into songs and those he couldn't. "The skill slipped from me in the pell-mell of grihasthi," he would say to me. One winter evening, he and I crouched beside a small fire at the boundary of our field. The crop was ripe and nilgai and black deer were roaming in the area. They could destroy the labour of six long months in the six brief hours of night, so we were guarding the field until the maize was ready for harvesting. "Let me tell you a story I have never told anyone else," he said.

'He couldn't say for sure where he had heard the story or whom he had heard it from, but he had known it a long time, perhaps forever. It was the story of a princess of celestial beauty and her unsuccessful suitors. "This story is not for everyone, and the Princess does not appear before everyone. But she appeared to me in my dream once. It was like a hundred diyas were lit inside of me, and instead of blood, my veins were filled with her beauty. I learnt to play music and make songs so I could sing her praises," my father told me. "She lives towards the west, safe in her tree, and when I was young, I wanted to find the tree and possess the Princess." "Why didn't you?" I asked. "Because I married your mother and forgot the path to the tree," he answered. "The Princess would not come in my dreams any more. Now I barely remember her features, but sometimes her dhani lehenga and kasumal odhani, the curve of her waist like the bend of a river, and her hands like lotus flowers when the sun shines on them, float before my eyes. I am one of her unsuccessful suitors too. One who couldn't even reach her presence," my father lamented.'

That day, the Sarangiya vowed that he would find the Princess, defeat the magic of the tree and make her his own. He must have been a mere boy of eleven or twelve, but he was determined. He acquired every skill to win the Princess over. But she did not appear to him, nor could he find her tree.

That dry Ashadh, he had finally learnt the way to her tree from some nomads, and was going to find her before Chaumaas ended. 'But she came to me herself,' he would say in wonder as we sat around our fire at night, 'when I was losing my senses and I was unable to recall a single note or word, when I had almost forgotten who I was.' He shook his head in bewilderment.

All through our journey, he described the Princess to me, her beauty, her pride, the clothes she wore, her exquisite ornaments. 'Come with me. I am going to the tree where she lives watched over by her warring suitors,' he said. 'I will know the tree by the red, shining rock near it, and the river singing under the desert sands. Perhaps you will see her too.

She will show herself to you and change the world for you.' But I am a Rabari, I can't leave my children, my camels. So the Sarangiya went away alone.

For many Saavans after that, I returned to the village by the big baoli and played hymns in Bhaumiya-ji's honour on my ravanhatha.

The Sarangiya still comes to our settlement sometimes. His hair has turned white like the silk-cotton of the semal tree, and his face is like a map of pain. But his eyes still have a hungry glare – he is waiting for the Princess to reveal herself again.

VI

EXCERPTS FROM THE COLLECTOR'S JOURNAL

2 May 19__

I'm touring my district. I think only so much can be achieved from the HQ. The organized hierarchy and systems of the HQ firmly trap and stymie everyone and everything. I try to break the trap, unsettle routines, unhinge protocols. I go to dhanis, villages, remote settlements, tehsil offices without much notice, and everywhere I go, I find that much needs to be done.

I left the HQ after lunch today and drove through the desert, dazzling in the heat like a sea of motionless, golden waves and reached the Circuit House this evening. Mathura's face was a picture of suffering resignation when he saw the long, low building of the dak bangla, as he calls it, with a deep veranda running along its length. Like numerous other

Circuit Houses around the state, and indeed the country, this too was built before Independence. There are some interesting natural features around it though, which I have not seen elsewhere in the desert. There's a large smooth rock, almost the size of a small hill, with curious, copper-coloured streaks, not far from the Circuit House compound. There is also a beautiful shade-tree in the compound. In this dry landscape with no visible source of water, this solitary tree, green and flourishing, is remarkable. It is not one of the common desert trees either, like *Prosopis cineraria* or acacia or trees of the *Ficus* family which grow in these parts. Its trunk is smooth, its leaves glossy and gently tapering. I have asked the staff of the Circuit House, but they don't know anything about it, neither its name nor its age. The guard of the place is the oldest staff member around here. He is a picturesque Bhil, six feet something, with snowy moustaches upturned and a hand-tied five-coloured turban on his head. He claims the tree was there when he served the British before Independence and was exactly the same, not a branch or a leaf less or more. As if he counts them daily! Teejan, who cooks at the Circuit House and has a turn of phrase as warm and crisp as the bejad rotis she makes, said it was a kalpavriksha. 'It grants boons,' she said. 'Just like the wishing tree which grows in the garden of Inder, the king of gods.' That means nothing, of course. Trees are the difference between life and death for desert folk and they tend to call any tree a kalpavriksha. I have heard Garasias use the term for the thorny khejri, more a shrub than a tree, and the Bishnois likewise for the *Ficus* trees. This one is probably some non-native perennial. I will examine it closely in a day or two, take leaf and bark samples to send for analysis.

Teejan has promised to bring dancers and musicians from her tribe over. She came out on to the veranda when I was playing my flute and, to Mathura's mute outrage, told me she liked my playing very much. Mathura is very proper, very concerned about my dignity. Though he never says so, he clearly believes that my indecorous behaviour, like talking to the kitchen staff or playing the flute without ordering everyone to stuff their ears shut, reflects discreditably on him. He is high-handed with the house staff, very dignified with district officers and smoothly respectful to me. He has the contempt of a dweller of the fertile plains towards the desert folk. Once, in an unusually loquacious moment, he told me that if people chose to live in a place fit only for scorpions, snakes and lizards when the whole world was open to them, they must have been born half-witted. I don't think he enjoys our tours much.

4 May 19—

Went around the tehsil. It is a poor land, no oasis around, no perennial source of water, the fields perpetually parched. And yet, nomads have settled here. They must have crossed the desert chasing shade and found it, scant as it is, beneath the clusters of khejri, babool, keekar and taad trees. They have been living here for generations, growing whatever they can, grazing their cattle in gauchar land and bearing the brunt of petty officialdom. Yet, these tribals are proud. They have more pride than the tehsil officials who treat them like dirt but grovel before even Mathura.

The dhanis here are to be seen to be believed. The huts are small and are built in neat little clusters with whatever is handy – mud, cow dung, dried twigs and palm fronds. Their mud walls are decorated with murals from stories told in these parts, with turmeric or vermilion handprints of women and children. The women draw patterns on the floor with lime and red clay, a different one for each festival. These clusters of grass-and-mud huts are often screened by the dunes completely. You need to climb the soft sand slopes or descend into troughs to discover them. At times, what you take for a ripple in the sand detaches itself and rises, and you see that it is actually a camel's hump, and at others, what looks like a rounded mud roof turns out to be a dune. The desert mirage is real here. And the ever-shifting landscape of the Thar means that when I look for a dhani I visited a week ago, I am unable to find it because the wind has shifted the dune I had used as a landmark. But the Tehsildar and the Patwaris and Ameens can find it without difficulty.

Like everyone in the desert, the dhani folk around here too keep goats and camels, except fewer, for the trees are meagre and everything depends on the capricious desert rains. Yet you hear strains of the algoza and desert flute, and men and women go about their work humming to themselves even in the hottest part of the afternoon. Most of the dhani folk ferment jaggery and grain in earthen pots buried deep in the sand, the location of each pitcher marked carefully with a twig. They are often bitten by scorpions and snakes that nest near the pitchers of taadi for warmth. It is, of course, not legal to make liquor – but who is to grudge them a few pitchers consumed mostly on festival days? They have a unique sense of beauty. The women embroider in bright colours and bold motifs. Their clothes are encrusted with mirrors and baubles, the harnesses and saddles of their camels are plaited with beads and coloured threads. Even the cloth ring on which the water pitchers are carried are worked with elaborate designs, long strings of beads hanging from them.

5 May 19—

Visited the tehsil office. The usual disarray – missing or mutilated records, no one remembers when the last land measurements were done, khasras incomplete, disputes over khata details unresolved for generations. I told the Tehsildar that I planned to hear petitions at the Circuit House starting tomorrow. His reaction was per usual too – there were no real disputes, the tribespeople made them up, they were all greedy and dishonest, the tribes they belonged to had a tradition of crime and prostitution. I told him all this had nothing to do with land records, that he better send notice to the dhanis and villages. I told him I would also visit a few dhanis on my way back to the Circuit House and spread the word. I expected him and the petitioners from eight o'clock onwards the next morning – this in my most stern Collector's tone. And while he was grappling with this, I closed with a final sortie – I asked Mathura to take the disputed records I was examining to the jeep. I will study them in the evening, I am sure Tehsildar Saheb will not mind! I left what remained of the poor Tehsildar behind in the tehsil office and turned back towards the Circuit House, visiting as many hut-clusters along the way as I could.

I stopped for a late lunch at one of the clusters, where two girls, clearly sisters, with skin like the velvet desert night and eyes like pairs of fluttering birds, were plaiting a rope from a spool of jute under the khejri trees. Their mother sat nearby, cleaning bajra. She had the same eyes and could not have been more than forty, but she was wrinkled and slack like a woman twenty years older. In the desert, age is not measured in the number of years one has lived but the number of years one has suffered. They were Nats, hospitable like all desert folk. They brought out buttermilk and goat's milk, jowar rotis and garlic chutney, and onions buried underground to preserve their juicy freshness. The mother mentioned a land demarcation dispute with the tehsil authorities. She went into the hut and roused her husband, but he was a cipher, drunk and gross. I told her to come the next day to the Circuit House and bring the relevant papers. Mathura stood pointedly apart all through, declining food, ignoring the interested looks the two girls cast at him, silently disapproving!

6 May 19—

After dinner last night, Teejan came up to me. 'My people are here,' she said, pointing to the colourful crowd in the courtyard, 'and some from other tribes too. They all want to dance for you. Turn your chair that way, Saheb, and we will dance in front of the wishing tree, and pray for all your desires to be fulfilled.'

I am still steeped in that spontaneous performance – the desert lutes, algoza and kamaycha are playing, the morchang and kartals are pounding, the dancers are swaying like trees. The Nat girls in their tight-fitting bodices and swirling lehengas ripple sensuously, as the singers sing about an armlet that has come loose, urging the hero to come and mend it and, along with it, the heart of his beloved. These scenes, like Rajasthani miniature paintings, beautifully detailed and colourful, play before my eyes as I work, resolving disputes, answering petitions all through the long day.

The durbar, as these problem-solving sessions are called in a throwback to colonial times, was packed as always. The veranda and the front courtyard were full of people too, a number of them had come to merely bow their turbaned heads and say 'ghani khamma' when they caught my eye. They always bring gifts – dried beans and berries, hand-crushed bajra and other millets, camel's milk and articles made of camel hair, mirror-work, beads. I asked one of my ADMs and Mathura to enter everything into a register and pay a fair price then and there. I have learnt from experience that leaving it until later does not work. Mathura always manages to keep the gifts but lose the people who brought them.

I disposed the land dispute of the Nat family from yesterday, but the girls did not leave with their mother. I saw them sitting in the shade of the tree and called them in. Turns out they know a sarangi player, a real artist from the tradition of the kingly courts. Could they bring him? Of course! And would I be generous in tipping him? This, with shrewdness in their lively eyes. Again, of course! I look forward to some more music tomorrow evening. This evening, I make do with some excellent ker sangri, spicy like a pickle, and kadhi made from fresh-ground gram flour and yoghurt, and the indescribable camel-milk kheer.

8 May 19—

My head is still swimming with the music the Sarangiya played the past two evenings.

When the Nat girls brought the white-haired sarangi player, his face creased and burnt by the desert sun, I expected the usual music of the Sindhi sarangi – a high-pitched, reverberating beauty accompanying the tales of valour of Amar Singh Rathod, Rana Sanga and Ratan Singh. But the Sarangiya is matchless, a musician like no other. His sarangi is a part of him, his second tongue, more melodious than any human voice. It responds to his bow and fingers and tells stories on its own, as if it were alive – which, of course, it is. The dead wood and metal and leather all quickened to life under the Sarangiya's touch. He wouldn't give his name, age or tribe, loftily claiming that his instrument was his name, that he was as old as naad, the original sound of the universe, and his tribe was love, the heavenly twin of music. I think he must belong to the musically gifted Langa or Manganiyar tribes. He is undoubtedly a superior performer. He was very pleased by my accompanying him on my flute. 'You are a brother artist. You performed for me,' he said and his eyes shone. 'I will give you something unique, a tale heard by but a few.' I await the evening eagerly.

10 May 19__

I have had an experience last evening. No, wrong. I have been going through an experience since yesterday evening. I will try to set it down here.

I finished dinner and was waiting for the Sarangiya, trying the compositions I had heard in the last couple of days on my flute, when suddenly he was there, under the tree. I had not seen him approach. The moon had just risen and the shade of the tree had a glowing, silvery quality. The Sarangiya seemed made of light and shade too. He called to me, 'Come Saheb, this is the right time, the right place, and you are the right recipient for the story. It must not be told to the wrong person, it cannot be poured into the wrong vessel.' I descended from the veranda. The Sarangiya turned and sat facing the tree and I sat next to him on the sand. He touched the sarangi to his forehead and, placing the goatskin-and-wood belly of the instrument on his knee, touched the strings with his bow. The sarangi responded.

O, the Princess was beautiful, kings and princes and common men alike wooed her, sang the Sarangiya. Her complexion was like an Ashadh morn, her eyes like nights in Saavan, like a rainbow she was slender, like a rain cloud voluptuous. In seasons, she was Paavas, in flowers, the scented chameli, among birds, she was the swan, and among women, she was Padmini of perfect beauty. The sun and the moon rose to look upon her and the rains washed her tresses. The night descended in her hair and the dawn rose from her lotus feet.

The sarangi now joined in. O, the Princess was beautiful, and none could bear to look upon her. She dazzled them by raising her eyes and plunged them into despair by averting them. The kings and princes and common men all wanted her to be theirs, but she lived in her high palace, away from everyone. She seldom came to her windows, rarely allowed the music of her voice to fall into yearning ears.

Then one day, the Sarangiya intoned in his voice like the wind among dunes, a mighty prince arrived. His chest was broader than the Aravallis and his arms longer than the branches of the vat tree. His charger stamped its copper feet under the high palace and sent up a shower of sparks to the Princess's window. The Princess appeared. What do you seek, she asked. I have come to win you, Princess, you shall be the queen of the earth, and pearls from the seas and rubies from the mountains will be crushed to make the pathway in your kesar kyaari, your saffron garden. The moon will be lustreless before the glow of your nath, and the fires of our passion will quell the sun.

As the Princess stood listening, a Siddha, one with powers honed through terrible penance, arrived. He was impervious to heat and cold and hunger – he had fasted for a decade, eating only the grain dropped by ants, and for another drinking only the raindrops which fell when the constellation Swati was in the sky. He glowed with powers like a second sun. He called out to the Princess – Give me what I ask for, O Princess. I want you. Descend into my arms from your high palace. The new moon shall be your hansuli and the seven stars your waistband. Belonging to me, you will attain supreme joy.

The Princess heard them both, her face averted. Come back after nine days and nine nights, she said to them, and you shall have my answer.

The sarangi picked up the tale here. On the tenth day, the suitors arrived. I want you both, the Princess said, and yet neither. You seek too much and yet too little. You give nothing. Go back to where you came from. She closed her casement and her laughter fell like fireworks from the sky. But the Siddha and the Prince did not wish to go back to their abodes. In truth, they could not go back, they had both forgotten the way. The Siddha let out an angry roar and the great domes of the high palace crashed to the ground. The Prince smote the foundations with his fist and the walls of the high palace buckled. The Princess fled, crossing the palace moat, running like the desert wind through the dunes until she could run no longer. The suitors drew closer and halted before the Princess. Then they turned on each other, fighting with weapons and enchantments. The Prince transformed into a mighty river and tried to drown the Siddha, whereupon the Siddha became a great rock and stemmed the flow of the river.

The Princess, who was watching, appealed to the desert and the sky – shelter me like mother and father, for I have vowed not to belong to any one. The desert and the sky heard her prayer and fashioned a beautiful tree. Its trunk was smooth as a child's cheek and its leaves were like lapises and emeralds. Into this radiant tree the Princess entered, baffling both the men. In vain did they rage and try to break the enchantment. The Prince, still in the form of a river, sank underground, and to this day waters the golden roots of the tree, hoping to win her. And the Siddha, in the form of a great rock, entered samadhi, still hoping to own her.

The Sarangiya stopped here. His sarangi's refrain hung in the air for a few moments, then all fell silent.

'What an intriguing tale, and how beautifully you have told it,' I said.

The Sarangiya looked at me. His eyes reflected the full moon, the colour of the Rajasthani kansa platter. 'This is not a fanciful tale. That is the Princess's tree, the Sundari Sankalp tree.'

'The beauty's vow tree? Is that what it is called?'

The Sarangiya looked at the tree, his eyes brimming. Tears fell. 'Yes,' he said, 'that's what it should be called. I saw the Princess once, when I was a young man. I have tried many times since, but she has never revealed herself again. Perhaps you will be luckier, perhaps you shall see her tonight.'

Involuntarily, my eyes turned towards the tree. A bronze moon hung above it and the entire tree glowed like a jewelled thing. It was then that I saw her. She stood near the tree, so near she might have been hewn from it. She wore a kanchali of some fine material. I could see her rounded breasts through it. Her midriff was bare and the palm of her left hand rested on the perfect curve of her waist. With her right hand she held up the folds of her lehenga, tied with a gold waistband just below her deep navel. Broad anklets circled her bare feet, the left one raised as if she were stepping down. The breeze stirred the leaves, and in the delicate moonlight her face glowed. Her eyes, like no other eyes I have seen, the pearl in her nose, her full lips dark like grapes, all gleamed with a perfection of lines and hues. She was the very essence of all that is beautiful. As she stood revealed, everything ceased to exist – the moon, the dunes, the music of the sarangi.

I rose and went to her. A chunari, thin as a spider's web, covered her tangled hair and trailed on the ground. My foot trod upon it. She turned her neck and her gaze fell upon me like daggers of ivory and opal. She threw her head back and ... was gone ... My life drained from my veins ... I could not move and fell on my hands and knees. I could not see, I could not breathe. Some animal of the desert uttered despairing cries, the air shattered like glass and pierced every particle of my body...

The Sarangiya raised me with his rough hands, helped me sit up against her tree. He took out his chillum, filled and lighted it, held it against my lips until I took a drag. Slowly, I stopped trembling. Silence descended.

The Sarangiya said eventually, 'You saw her right enough and I, sitting here with you, couldn't. Was she dressed in green? Was she holding her odhani between her teeth? Was her ghaghra tied with a gold kardhani?'

'I remember the gold waistband,' I said, 'and her eyes ... She looked at me.'

'You are fortunate, Saheb. She never looks at anyone, just keeps her head averted.'

'Where is she now? Where did she go?' I held on to the Sarangiya's arm.

'She is here. Her beauty is dispersed in everything. When she chooses, she concentrates it and reveals herself. You are fortunate,' he repeated, then helped me up. 'Rest, Saheb. You have seen her, she has looked at you, that is bliss enough.' I tried to give him everything in my pocket, but he refused. 'You can't give me anything. Money does not repay the debt I have placed you under.' Bowing, he walked away into the desert.

Eventually, I went to my room, lay in my bed. But how could I rest? The eyes flashed before me again and again, the delicate neck was drawn back and she was gone, again and again and again, in an endless cycle. I could not bear it any longer. I went out, sat by the tree and pleaded with her.

3 June 19__

Days have passed. Initially, it surprised me that the days followed each other without break. With passing time, however, my certainty that I saw her, the Princess, under her tree, is eroding. Was it a fancy, a trick of light and shadow? Was she there? And yet, her eyes look at me and again I feel the stillness, the breath leaving my body, all things dissolving into a blankness that frames her and her alone. She is the only being in the gaping void.

18 June 19__

I returned to the Circuit House three days ago. The moon was bright and high. I need to see her again, even if just once, even if for a brief moment. I go to her every night, pleading on my knees, grovelling on the ground before her. I want to see you, I need to, I must have sight of you again, for my sanity and for your verity, see my need and come to me. Mathura has been setting up a camp cot by her side for me. Days are spent in work, people from other tehsils have heard of my camping at the Circuit House and come here with their problems. I have asked one of my ADMs to join me here from tomorrow as well. I am determined to stay until she shows herself.

22 June 19__

There is no point to anything any more. I stay up night after night, pleading with a vision. The staff think I am crazy. The other day, I overheard the cook say to Mathura that I smoke ganja. The reality of dreams is clashing with the dream of reality. I have to go away, break this cycle, wake up. I have to reconnect before I drift away any further. I have decided to go to Delhi – to old friends, to Abha. I have been cryptic in my letters to her, neglecting to reply to the long ones she writes regularly. The books and magazines she sends lie unopened, but I will make amends. Abha has been patient, waiting these two years, seeing me only occasionally when I have returned for brief periods, never complaining. I have applied for leave and will hand over the district to my SDM as soon as my application is approved.

30 July 19—

I returned yesterday to the HQ, five days before my leave ends. Going away resolved nothing. No, that's wrong, it has resolved everything – it is clear to me that I must offer myself to her. I can only seek her by losing myself. I have made excuses to Ma and Daddy, to family, friends. I have left them baffled, angry, hurt. Everyone found me absent, distracted when I was there. How come you are so disinterested, my friends asked over and over again, you have become part of the establishment, you have sold out, given up, you are no longer incisive, subversive. They addressed me as Collector Saheb derisively and dismissed me.

And Abha ... I tried to be at the place Abha and I were before I took charge of my district, before I experienced the desert, before I saw her ... I tried to be together with Abha, in our ideas and concerns, wishes and desires. But it is futile. After the problems I have handled, problems of life and death, hunger, money, land, hardships of body and soul which the desert people accept as a matter of course, the world of ideological points and theoretical debates which she and my friends inhabit seems like make-believe, like precocious children playing with subtle toys. We failed to meet in every way. I failed. She, the one who cannot be denied, stood in the way...

My last evening in Delhi we went to Embassy. We ate mutton chops and chicken Stroganoff and handmade ice cream. And we talked. It felt like old times and yet not quite ... The brown irises of Abha's eyes were liquid, a familiar look in them. 'I have missed you,' she said, 'do you understand? Missed being close, your arms around me, the intimacy. I have needed you so much.' 'I thought you were completely self-sufficient, you had everything in hand,' I joked feebly. 'There is only so much I can do for myself,' she laughed. After dinner, we went to her place. Her family was away. 'They have gone to Rishikesh, to pray for a groom for me.' Her eyes shone in the half-gloom of the small lobby. We entered the dimly lit living room. Abha turned to me. 'Hold me, please,' she murmured. I felt my blood well up. I held her close, pressing her to me, her soft, rounded body, beautiful, known, not a mirage, resting in my arms. I closed my eyes and kissed her, caressing her back, hooking a finger in the strap of her bra through her blouse. The free end of her sari slipped to the floor. Abha sighed, her body relaxed in my arms. 'I have missed you,' she whispered again and again, her warm mouth on my ear, her fingers fluttering on my face, my neck. She leaned back slightly and loosened her blouse, took my hand and placed it on her breast. I could feel the rhythm of her heart. Warmth swirled inside me. This was real. I opened my eyes and leaned into Abha.

Suddenly the room lit up with a silver flash, and I saw her. Her eyes were averted this time, no headscarf, hair over her shoulders, her bare, golden back turned towards me, the silken cords of her kanchali tied in knots across it, the long, free ends beaded with pearls, emeralds and rubies falling to her hips. My eyes were dazzled. I couldn't see anything but her glowing form. I only wanted to see her, hold her. 'Princess,' I called, 'Princess,' and reached for her. There was an obstruction in my way ... Abha ... Or was it my own self? I couldn't think any more. The need to reach her, to be held by her, burned in me. She stood for a moment in the centre of the room, in the centre of the world gone still and silent, in the centre of my being and ... was gone.

Everything drained away, I was sightless, stripped of volition, thrown into a limitless emptiness. All was extinguished for me. It was death, but with no end. She was gone. Abha was angry, hurt, confused ... There were tears, accusations, but I could do nothing. Nothing. I couldn't soothe her pain, I couldn't explain myself. In the end, I left.

The pull is relentless, inexorable. I have cut all ties. Now I must go to her without conditions or needs, go with my own soul as an offering, implore her to take it, take me. I have accepted that I have no other option.

1 August 19__

I am here. I know she is here too. Earlier this evening, Mathura had asked whether it was a daura. I like the word, it is the right word, it means both a tour and a bout of madness. Perhaps this is both. But, no, after coming here, I feel the certainty of her presence. The dream is real, there is no other reality. Everything else is a dream, seen in the somnambulist state I have lived in for so long. I am awake now. I am going to meet her tonight, under the finely etched moon of the fourth night of Shravan. She will have fragrant mehndi on the palms of her hands and red lac bangles on her arms. I will go to her now.

2 August 19__

She came last night. This is bliss, the hollow inside me is filled. I feel alive like never before, alert to every sensory experience. I can see the rays of the sun distinct from one another, the individual grains of sand forming the dunes, I can smell the top note and base of the incense stick the cook has lit in the kitchen, hear the liquid gargle of the tea being poured and the gentle splash when the stream hits the cup. I am able to see all – the parts and the whole, at the same time. Her beauty has brought complete harmony.

Last night, I played the flute, I played her song. O Princess of great beauty, whose eyes slay and succour, I have come to you to surrender my very being, I want to belong to you, you have won me and you must own me. I was calm as I breathed the words in the flute, a prayer to her because, clad in her fragile beauty, she is the mightiest. And she came! She sat by me on the camp cot, held me in her arms as the moonlight holds the desert. She allowed me to tumble her hair about, suckle at her breast, kiss her navel and gently remove her gold waistband. The desert and the sky witnessed our union, joy ascended to the sky like incense smoke, dropped like nectar on the golden body of the desert. As the morning star set, she touched my face with her hands like blue lotuses, kissed me with lips fragrant like jasmine, and was gone.

She will return tonight, her smell, the smell of the parijat, is infused in me. She has made me hers. I will go to work now. And as I work, her tree will be visible from my window. My brain is so clear, so lucid – it's as if I have been reborn.

VII

THE MEDICAL OFFICER'S SUMMARY NOTE

I HAVE NOW BEEN WITH the Collector of __ district for a little over two weeks. During this time, I have interviewed a number of people, including the Collector himself, in order to understand the cause of his delusion. That he suffers from a delusion is, of course, without doubt. It is manifest in his apparent and continued belief, in the face of contrary evidence, in things which cannot be seen or verified, and thus, from a scientific point of view, do not exist. From the information at hand, it would appear that the physical effect of the alternating dry heat and cold of the desert and his extreme exertions in touring the district, the potential neural and emotional effects of the music and, above all, the adverse effect of long isolation in the desert on a sensitive temperament have all contributed to his present condition.

It is regrettable that the sarangi player could not be located. I believe he could have thrown light on specific points of the Collector's narration as he was present at the time the delusion first manifested itself. Valuable information on the circumstances of that night could have been gleaned from interviewing him. From, in particular, the accounts of the camel-herder and the guard of the Circuit House, I am inclined to suspect the sarangi player himself suffers from a psychological condition. His extreme pride points to a narcissistic personality disorder and, by all accounts, he seems to suffer from a delusion similar to the Collector's. This may well be a case of one individual who suffers from multiple psychological conditions inducing delusions or hallucinations in others under certain circumstances – a phenomenon observable in leaders of cults and other movements, religious or secular, who are purported to induce visions or revelations in their disciples. His so-called acts of magical cures and paranormal manifestation point to this hypothesis as well. In brief, an examination of the sarangi player would have been invaluable in researching mental conditions.

I have spent hours reasoning with the Collector about his claims of a princess of extraordinary beauty residing in the tree. It is plain to all that the tree is an ordinary tree, and the princess he describes is no different from the folk heroines of tales told by bards and lyricists in Rajasthan, depicted in innumerable miniatures in palaces and havelis, which he must have seen during his travels through the desert. He, however, persists in his delusion. I have to note here his ability to marshal cogent, plausible arguments supporting the fanciful story narrated by the sarangi player. He has caused scientific investigations to be conducted on certain points of the narrative and has obtained proof that appears to support the story. Geophysicists have found an underground water source with large amounts of water in the area around the tree. The water is sweet – a rarity in this desert where all water is hard and full of salt. The rock, too, he has had examined. Geological reports, which I have had the opportunity to review, have identified signs of water erosion on it. Scientists have been unable to identify the origin of the rock. It does not appear to them to be from the desert, nor does it have any similarities with those found in the mountain ranges of this region. He has shown me his correspondence with botanists who have been unable to categorize the tree in any particular genus and species. They have suggested it could be a hybrid with connections to the prolific *Ficus* family, particularly in its glossy, tapering leaves and its perennial character. I have put forward the suggestion that the tree is perhaps the outcome of a grafting by some English officer interested in botany, but the Collector does not accept it. He does not allow anyone to touch the tree and would not permit me to take samples of its leaves, bark or root tissues. This is the one point on which he becomes singularly agitated, which leads me to the apprehension that his delusion at some point may turn into a full-blown psychosis.

In my professional opinion, though, at this point he is competent to discharge his duties, which, based on my independent observation, he performs very well, with efficiency and genuine regard for the well-being of the people of his district. He is clearly a gifted and dedicated administrator. The work he has initiated to utilize the underground water for supplying nearby villages, and the land reforms he has commissioned across the district have caused tangible improvement in the lives of the villagers and nomads. He has petitioned to be permitted to continue residing at the Circuit House in __ tehsil and working from there instead of the district headquarters. In view of his present condition, in my professional opinion, that would be the best course – as any attempt to dislodge him from the vicinity of the tree may tip the balance over and trigger a mental crisis. In layman's terms, I recommend humouring him in his request.

VIII

NOTATION BY THE CHIEF SECRETARY

Mr __, the collector of district __, has submitted a petition to me requesting the relocation of the district headquarters to the Circuit House in tehsil __. Even before the petition, I was aware of the rather unorthodox way in which the DC had been operating in his district. The Tehsildar of tehsil __ had submitted his own petition on the matter of conducting district business from the Circuit House in his tehsil. He had written in detail about the breakdown in administrative hierarchy in the tehsil and the issues created by frequent durbars for nomads held at the Circuit House by the DC.

After receipt of the petition, I separately consulted with the district officials to fully understand the matter on hand. In my discussions, certain information emerged which suggested the need to obtain a medical report on the DC, with particular reference to his mental condition. I, therefore, instructed the Medical Officer, Dr __, to examine the DC and submit a complete report, which he did and which I have perused.

Whilst I commend the thoroughness with which the MO approached the matter and the time he spent in examining the DC, I must note that in my view the discussions with nomads and Class 4 staff were hardly needed or desirable. I regret that I cannot strike those accounts and parts of the DC's journal, another needless document, from the file, as they are appended as annexures to the note submitted by the MO. Accordingly, these documents, so unsuitable for government records for a number of reasons, will regretfully remain part of the DC's confidential file. I shall, however, neither dwell on them nor take them into consideration for the purpose of this note and my decision.

The only germane part of the MO's report is his note on the DC's health and fitness, where he has confirmed that the DC is competent and, indeed, excels in discharging his official duties. As the instruction to the MO was to submit a report on the mental fitness of the DC and no view was sought from him on the DC's petition, I shall also disregard his recommendation in this regard and examine the DC's petition on its merits alone.

In his written submission, the DC has given a number of reasons for his request to move the headquarters of the district to the Circuit House in tehsil __. He has also met me on one occasion to present the matter and further elucidate the reasons detailed in his petition. There is no need to dwell on the DC's personal preference for the Circuit House in question – it is amply demonstrated by the long duration of time he has been camping there. I shall, therefore, now review objectively the reasons cited in his application.

The main reasons stated in the submission by the DC are:

1. The project for the exploitation of underground water resources which he has initiated and which requires close supervision.
2. The land record amendments which require his continued presence in the mofussil.
3. The relative location of the Circuit House in tehsil __ being more central than the present district headquarters.

I shall begin with the last reason first, as the DC has cited it as a fundamental reason for the long-term relocation of the district headquarters. In fact, during his meeting with me, he drew, in freehand, a fairly accurate map of his district, demarcated the tehsils, and plotted the positions of the district headquarters and the Circuit House in tehsil __ to demonstrate that the Circuit House is indeed located more centrally. He stated that relocating the district headquarters will help in the balanced development of the district. According to him, several large villages in and around tehsil __, in particular __ Palani, __ ki Dhani, Kalan __, etc., have the potential to become centres of tourism and desert trade. He believes that the shift of the district headquarters is, therefore, a logical move.

Here, I must note my astonishment at the argument the DC has made. He very well knows that districts are demarcated by the legislative arm of the government and a shift of district headquarters has implications that are not just administrative but also political. To advocate such moves without due consideration to such implications, merely because they are logical, shows a lack of understanding of the complexity of administration. Administration is not run by logic. There are other factors to be considered as well. It is noteworthy that the argument of 'central location' could be made for the relocation of the capitals of several states, and indeed of the national capital itself!

Therefore, whilst I do not disagree with the factual part of the DC's representation that the Circuit House in tehsil __ is centrally located and relocating the district headquarters could lead to development of the surrounding area, I am unable to accord it any weight, as such a relocation will be disruptive of the current set-up.

With regard to the remarkable work the DC has done in his district to resolve land title disputes and improve record-keeping, I have only commendations to offer. The revenue collection in his district has increased and instances of default have fallen. His work is a model for other districts. However, whilst this work currently requires his visiting different tehsils and areas of his district, it does not necessitate moving the district headquarters permanently.

The one reason that is material in the submission is the water distribution project which is under way, and which is indeed important and has far-reaching impact. Given the scale of the project and its potential significance for the state, I believe currently there is benefit in the DC himself supervising it. It is also apparent that the Circuit House is ideally located for the purpose of establishing a project office for the canal and other related works that are under way. It is my belief that once the initial phase of the project is completed and its benefits are apparent, the immediate supervision work may be handed over to more junior officers. The DC has himself estimated the initial phase to take nine to twelve months to complete. I, therefore, approve his continuing to operate from the Circuit House for the above period.

Separately, I also recommend transferring the DC to a new posting thereafter. He is an able administrator and has the ability to do much good in other parts of the state. The childish fable of the tree princess, which so impressed the MO and which the DC alluded to in our meeting is, in my view, the result of associating with common mendicants of the desert. A change of scene, which a new posting would necessarily entail, will rid him of the strange idea.

IX

FINAL REPORT ON THE DISTURBING HAPPENINGS IN ___ TEHSIL, BY THE SENIOR SUPERINTENDENT OF POLICE

INITIAL INFORMATION REGARDING THE happenings at the Circuit House was received by my staff late on the evening of __ March. One of the Naib Tehsildars called to report that there was a big crowd at the Circuit House. He also said that the Tehsildar had been behaving in a strange manner all morning, muttering to himself, refusing to step outside the tehsil office and eventually locking himself in his cabin. He further reported that, around noon, the Tehsildar burst out of his cabin and left the tehsil office. The Naib Tehsildar who reported the matter seemed more puzzled than alarmed, and my Inspector who received the message did not consider it a serious matter as the Station House Officer of the tehsil had not reported anything untoward. The next morning, the SHO reported large numbers of villagers and nomads gathering in the tehsil. He said that the crowd was at least twice as big as that at the camel fair and people were still pouring in. He hadn't been able to contact the Tehsildar in spite of every effort. I instructed him to investigate. However, before the SHO could provide further information on the situation, I received orders from the headquarters to ascertain the state of affairs at the Circuit House and report back. I understood that efforts to establish communication with the Circuit House had failed and I decided to proceed there immediately.

My initial instructions were to obtain a full understanding of the situation and ensure that law and order was maintained. The canal and the newly built rail tracks were to be protected from damage at all costs, and a report submitted to the headquarters at the earliest.

I assembled my officers and constables, and departed for the Circuit House within an hour of receiving the instructions, arriving by late evening. The surrounding area was dotted with cooking fires and lanterns. There were makeshift camps all around, and a number of camel carts and a few tractor trolleys could be seen. Goats and children ran about, strains of music could be heard, and the whole atmosphere was not unlike that of a desert fair. I drove up to the Circuit House with some difficulty, not because the gathered villagers offered any resistance but because of their sheer number. I estimated the number of people gathered there to be between ten and fifteen thousand. For a sparsely populated tehsil in the heart of the Thar desert, that is a large number, easily greater than the population of all the nearby villages put together. The compound of the Circuit House itself was so full of people that we had to alight from the jeeps at the gate itself. The activity in the compound seemed to be intense, with people gathered at the northern end. Parties of singers were singing, beating small brass cymbals, and men and women – tribals by the look of them – were dancing.

My men spread out and I entered the Circuit House. Though the compound and surrounding area were milling with people, the house itself was silent and appeared deserted. One of my constables finally brought a young man to me. He identified himself as the DC's orderly. His uniform was crumpled and his eyes red. I suspected he had been smoking ganja with the villagers camped outside. I questioned him on what was going on and why, instead of clearing the crowds, he seemed to have joined them. He wouldn't look at me. He shifted from foot to foot, and mumbled that the villagers were not doing any harm. His answering back in that vein to a superior was surprising, and I asked him whether the DC had approved the gathering. He appeared uncomfortable at the question. By this time, it was clear to me that the DC was not present in the Circuit House. I assumed that he was away on a tour or was at the district headquarters. Not wishing to waste any more time with the orderly, I asked him where the DC was. He looked even more uncomfortable at this and, muttering something, quickly stepped out of the room. My view at this stage was that the villagers, perhaps with the collusion of the Circuit House staff, had taken advantage of the DC's absence. From what I had observed so far, I was certain that the gathered villagers were not disorderly in conduct nor did they appear to harbour violent intentions. With the force I had with me, and the SHO and his team from the Station House, I did not consider their dispersal to pose any difficulty. The Circuit House staff's conduct, though inappropriate and in violation of service rules, I considered to be more appropriately addressed by the DC himself. To me, the questions that seemed to be pressing were: Why had the desert folk chosen this particular part of the desert to hold their revels, and how could I best disperse them in an orderly manner?

Next, I asked one of my constables to locate the Tehsildar and bring him to me. It was important to identify the leaders of the congregated villagers, and the Tehsildar was the man with local knowledge. However, before my man could leave, the orderly returned accompanied by the Tehsildar. Although I had met him on a few occasions, I could barely recognize him. He was a changed man, and appeared remarkably tense and restless. I put it down to the unprecedented situation in his tehsil and his natural apprehension of being held accountable for it. However, his full cooperation was necessary for a smooth handling of the situation and, in order to reassure him, I told him he had done the right thing by reporting the gathering to the headquarters. But this seemed to have an adverse effect on him and his agitation visibly increased. He looked over his shoulder wildly and clutched at the orderly's arm. Given that this was a Tehsildar with thirty years of experience and authority over the entire tehsil, I found his conduct unbecoming. I asked him sharply whether, besides reporting the matter to the headquarters, he had also informed the DC of the situation. He muttered that he had done nothing. In fact, his behaviour became increasingly extraordinary. Twitching his shoulders and swearing on every desert deity, he kept muttering that he had done nothing, nothing at all. Not informing the DC was a serious lapse on his part, and I told him so. At this, he seemed to lose whatever grip he had over himself. His eyes appeared to roll and his entire face twitched, he sweated profusely, all the while repeating like a mantra that he had made no reports, done nothing. I concluded that he was either mentally unstable or under the influence of some intoxicant.

I began suspecting that the matter went beyond the gathered villagers, and felt that the DC should be brought into the picture immediately. He was ultimately responsible for the district and the fact that no one had informed him of the situation was concerning. I asked the orderly: What was the matter with the Tehsildar, and where was his Saheb? At this point, a woman entered. From her dress and looks, she seemed to be from one of the nomadic tribes. She identified herself as Bhaagan and said she was from the nearby settlement of the Nat tribe.

I am setting below the ensuing conversation as closely as I can recollect, as this was the first account of the happenings at the Circuit House.

Bhaagan: You don't need to look for Collector Saheb. He has returned to the story he came from. The sarkar wanted him to leave this place where he'd brought such good times as had not been heard of since the reign of Pabu-ji himself. How could he go elsewhere? He knew that only he could rid us of our sufferings and bring sukaal to this desert.

SSP: What do you mean? What's sukaal?

Orderly: Don't pay any attention to what she says please, Sir. She is my woman. Collector Saheb looked after her tribe, and they think the land and good crops and water are all because of him.

Bhaagan: They are. The good times have come because of him, because of Sukaal Dev.

SSP: This makes no sense at all. Who is this Sukaal Dev? What is going on? Where is Collector Saheb?

Orderly: I don't understand it either, Sir. I can only say what I know.

SSP: Tell me all you know.

Orderly: My Saheb received the order for a new posting a few weeks ago. I heard of it from the ADMs who come to the dak bangla from the headquarters. 'Pack your things, Mathura,' they said to me. 'Your Saheb has got a big posting. You'll be leaving this place soon to go to a city.' I told Bhaagan here. You would understand, Sir, that I needed to ask her – this desert is her home, she was born here. So she said, 'Don't go.' I told her I can't leave my sarkari job and brew taadi like her father. So she said to me, 'Have you borrowed your tongue from someone, that you don't know how to use it? Ask Saheb to give you work at the canal. There are many good jobs there.' So I spoke to Saheb. I told him I couldn't leave.

SSP: Did Saheb mind that you did not wish to go with him? Was he angry with you?

Orderly: No, no, Sir, he just laughed. 'You used to count the days and couldn't wait to leave the desert,' he said to me, 'and now you don't want to go. Why, you could go to the cinema every day in the new place.' But he was joking. My Saheb knew all that was before Bhaagan. He knew everything. He was like a father and a mother to me. My own family cut me off when they heard that Bhaagan was from the Nat tribe. Only Saheb helped us. He paid for the wedding feast and summoned a pandit from the headquarters to marry us. We were married properly, in a proper ceremony with mantras and the holy fire as witness. She didn't just come to live with me with her cloth bundle and a bottle of desi daaru like women in her tribe do. I told Collector Saheb I wanted to serve him, but I needed to stay here. 'I too want to serve,' he said, 'and I too must stay here.'

SSP: What did he mean? He serves the government and has to go wherever he is posted.

Orderly: I don't know what he meant, Sir. He wasn't speaking to me, I could see he was talking to himself. Anyway, he spoke to the canal overseer and I got a job in my grade – same pay and I could stay in my quarters here at the dak bangla and look after my Saheb until he left for his new posting. The canal work is not far from here. Everything was going well. Every morning I made sure all was in order for my Saheb, and every evening I returned here and looked after him as usual. Then, two nights ago, he told me he didn't want any dinner and took his flute out to the tree.

SSP: At night? In this cold?

Orderly: Yes, Sir. He slept under that tree through all seasons. 'People have always slept in the open desert, be it winter, summer or rain,' he used to say. Though what are desert rains – just like a bird pissing ... Winters are harsh, but Bhaagan and her sister had woven new camel-hair blankets for him only last year, and I always brought out an angeethi to him under the tree. That night, too, I arranged his bed under the tree and placed the coal brazier, his slippers and a lamp beside it. Later, Teejan – she cooks here at the bangla – she told me Saheb hadn't eaten during the day either. But what could I do? What could I say to Saheb? I was not even his orderly any more – he had been assigned a new one in the city where his new posting was. That night, he was still playing his flute when Bhaagan and I went to our quarters at the back of the bangla. When I woke up the next morning, I heard his flute. Bhaagan did too, you can ask her. I said to her, 'Saheb is going to wear himself down like this, not eating, not sleeping.' She rightly told me to hurry up and prepare his breakfast. I took Saheb's tea and toast out to the tree, but he wasn't there ... And yet, I swear on my dead mother, Sir, I could hear his flute. It was as if he was there under the tree, playing his flute, but I couldn't see him ... Just like Kanamal used to say ... Despite my eyes, I was blind...

SSP: Are you out of your mind? Are you saying your Saheb became invisible? Did you try to look for him? Did you inform the Thanedaar? Send a message to the district headquarters?

Orderly: We looked for him everywhere around the dak bangla. Bhaagan and Teejan went round to their dhanis, the driver went to the nearby villages. But no one had seen him. We sent a message to the Tehsildar right away. He came around noon.

SSP: Tehsildar, you are the chief officer of the tehsil. Why this delay? Why did you not come immediately, or inform the headquarters or the Thanedaar? You left orderlies and drivers to run around on their own?

Bhaagan: Arre, Saheb, he came only when the Sarangiya went looking for him, the coward.

Tehsildar: He wouldn't let me ... The Sarangiya, he wouldn't let me make a report. Believe me, Saheb, he wouldn't ... He stood outside the tehsil office and glared at me. His eyes were of burning coal, he was clothed in a desert storm ... I begged him ... begged him ... Finally, he told me to pray ... to pray here. So I came ... My brain was struck by lightning, I had drunk the essence of dhatura flowers, that I thought of complaining to Chief Secretary Saheb about Collector Saheb ... about our Dev. Dev, forgive me. I am like your black cow, Dev...

SSP: Have you all gone out of your minds? Who is this Sarangiya? What is his connection with Collector Saheb?

Orderly: He ... he is a nomad, Sir. We don't know much about him. There are many nomads in the desert...

Bhaagan: But none like the Sarangiya. Mathura, your heart is like a fluttering peepul leaf. Why not speak about the Sarangiya? He did no wrong. Saheb, the Sarangiya is an old kalavant, he is peerless in the desert where musicians are as numerous as grains of sand. He used to come here often, but we haven't seen him in these parts for a long time now. A Rabari brought his sarangi here a few months ago and Saheb kept it in his own room. That morning, when Saheb turned into Dev, Mathura found the broken sarangi under the tree.

SSP: The Sarangiya came here the night the Collector went missing?

Orderly: I ... I don't know, Sir. We haven't seen the Sarangiya in almost two years ... But the sarangi was under that tree. Saheb couldn't have taken it down by himself, no one could. It was kept in a box Saheb got made especially for it, on top of the old almirah. I used to borrow the longest ladder from the canal works to reach it for dusting...

Tehsildar: He ... he came himself. He is created by the Devil's maya ... Ask the cook, ask the staff, ask that bewitched tree...

SSP: Stop this nonsense, all of you! Do you think I will believe these tales? You are all sarkari employees. You'll lose your jobs if you keep lying like this.

Bhaagan: Why would we lie? May our goats become barren and our fields yield thorns if we have uttered a word of untruth about our Dev.

Orderly: Shut your mouth, Bhaagan. I have told the truth, Sir, every word's true. None of us have seen the Sarangiya. The cook says he'd hear the sarangi playing in the compound many a night. And of course Kanamal, the guard of the bangla, he always speaks about the Sarangiya. But we haven't seen him.

SSP: Nonsense. The Collector must have found some other sarangi player to come here occasionally and play the sarangi for him.

Orderly: That is not possible, Sir. My Saheb would have mentioned it, someone would have seen the other player, and though I don't know anything about sarangi music, even I could tell the difference between the Sarangiya's playing and that of any other musician. You can ask Kanamal. He has heard him play for years. He always says there is no mistaking his sarangi – it is sweeter than any woman's voice.

SSP: None of this makes sense. Constable, tell Thanedaar Saheb that no one who was here the night the Collector was last seen is to leave the compound. Tomorrow morning, I want every one of them to report here.

Bhaagan: Don't worry, Saheb, all of us will remain here. We have vowed to pray at the Dev's thaan for seven days and seven nights.

SSP: Dev's thaan? There is a temple in the Circuit House? Is that why your people have gathered here?

Bhaagan: The dak bangla itself is a temple now. It is the thaan of our Sukaal Dev, our Saheb. He brought water and justice to this desert, and now he will remain here forever. And the good times he brought, they will remain too. Neither you nor your sarkar can take them away.

SSP: Take your woman away, Orderly, she is talking nonsense. Tomorrow morning, everyone should be here without fail. Constable, take down everyone's names and get someone to take the Tehsildar home too.

I have set all this down verbatim, or as close as possible, to highlight the state the Circuit House and tehsil staff were in, and the fantastical stories already in circulation regarding the fate of the Collector.

It was late and I wanted to consult with my SHO before questioning the staff more closely. I, therefore, dismissed everyone. The Tehsildar, who all through the above conversation was squatting on the floor like a common peasant, muttering and rocking back and forth, refused to go home. He appeared terrified at the prospect of leaving the Circuit House and prostrated himself on the ground. 'He will come after me,' he kept repeating. 'Here, Collector Saheb will save me.' I instructed the orderly to find him a bed and take care of him.

I took stock of the situation with my SHO. He is not a local man and was less unnerved by the events than others. He reported that when he had arrived at the Circuit House earlier that day, he had heard a rumour about the Collector turning into a god and entering the kalpavriksha. He stated that he had heard a lot of unbelievable and contradictory stories about the Collector in the past as well – that he summoned divine apsaras with his flute, that a mighty demon had brought water from the netherworld at his command, that he performed black magic, that he himself was under the influence of black magic ... The list was long. The SHO said that he, therefore, did not pay much attention to the tale. He had considered sealing off the area. However, by that time the crowd had already swelled into the thousands. He had rightly decided not to take the risk of provoking the villagers with his handful of constables, and had waited at the Circuit House for my unit to arrive. He had surveyed the area around the tree where the people were congregated, singing praises in honour of the newly anointed Dev, the District Collector. He showed exceptional sensibility in instructing his constables to remove their shoes and treat the area as sacred ground for the sake of the desert folk. He had found the Collector's bed, blanket, slippers and iron brazier under the tree, as well as the sarangi with the broken strings, and had taken them into his custody, assuring the leaders of the nomads that the objects would be treated like sacred relics. I instructed him to send messages to the state's control rooms along with a photograph of the Collector, and to dispatch the personal effects recovered from under the tree to the approved laboratory for testing. I also instructed him to let me know immediately if any information regarding the District Collector was received. Then, in view of the lateness of the hour, I dismissed everyone.

I should note that, at this stage, I did not suspect any foul play in relation to the DC's disappearance and fully expected him to turn up within the next couple of days. It is no secret that there had been rumours about the DC, who had been camping at the Circuit House for a long time. I, like many others, have heard about his examination by the District Medical Officer. Given his known peculiarities, I did not consider it entirely unrealistic that he might have decided to visit a far-flung settlement or accompanied a nomadic group to see some curiosity of the desert. I expected to hear some news of him by the next morning, and my primary concern at this stage was to counter the foolish story about him turning into a god and to tackle the crowds of tribesmen gathered at the Circuit House. In my years of service, I have seen that the imagination of desert folk is very vivid, perhaps to compensate for the barrenness of their land, and once a story like this takes root, it is difficult to dispel.

The next morning there was still no news about the DC. He had not made contact with the Secretariat or his staff at the district headquarters. His parents, in the meanwhile, had arrived in Jaipur and met with the Chief

Secretary. Newspapers had picked up the story and were painting the DC as some sort of folk hero. His so-called discovery of underground water was made much of, and there were questions tabled in the State Assembly about his disappearance. There was pressure to advance the investigation, and I conducted the first round of questioning of the Circuit House staff and other relevant sources myself. Nothing new emerged from these interviews. Most of the staff repeated versions of the story the orderly had told. The project officer and overseer from the nearby canal works confirmed that, though the camp buzzed with activity night and day, none of the workers or guards had reported anything untoward that night. According to them, no strangers had been sighted in the vicinity nor had the camp dogs barked that night. Interestingly, the cook denied having heard the sarangi that or any other night. He also denied any knowledge of the events that night and, in answer to every question, summoned God to be his witness and repeated that he always slept soundly. My SHO interrogated him thoroughly over a number of days, but he was unable to provide any meaningful information regarding the DC. However, he was able to clear up a few unsolved thefts at the Circuit House, and provided useful information on a smuggling operation that had been going on for a few years – he had been acting as a key link for smugglers on both sides of the border.

Some interesting information, muddled as usual with fantasy, came from the old guard of the Circuit House. Though his complete statement, along with those of the others, is part of the case file, I have extracted below certain parts of my interview with him for ease of reference.

SSP: Where were you the night Collector Saheb was last seen?

Guard: I was here, Hukum, guarding the gate. I am always here, there is nowhere else for me.

SSP: Did you notice anything unusual that night?

Guard: Nothing initially. As usual, Collector Saheb played his flute under the tree. It was cold, so Mathura brought the angeethi out. Later, Saheb spread his thick dohar on the ground and leaned against the tree trunk. After a while, the Sarangiya joined him and played his sarangi. Along with the tree, I too listened to their duet.

SSP: So the Sarangiya came to the Circuit House that night? Mathura and the rest say they haven't seen him for many months.

Guard: They tell the truth. They haven't seen him, yet he has been here.

SSP: How is that possible? Has he been hiding somewhere? Have you been helping him?

Guard: Everything is possible, Hukum. It is dark in the shade though the day is bright. There's rain in the desert for those who have seen it, but none for those who haven't.

SSP: Guard, have you gone mad? Speak clearly. This is a serious matter.

Guard: I am telling you, Hukum, the Sarangiya was here. I, Kanamal, with sight unlike anyone else's, saw him. Collector Saheb saw him. Even Tehsildar Saheb has seen him.

SSP: You make no sense, Guard. If the Sarangiya was here, where is he now?

Guard: He was here until that night. Where he is now, who can say? It was always difficult to know where he came from, where he went to. Now that he has discarded his chola, it is impossible to know.

SSP: You mean the Sarangiya is dead? When did he die? How?

Guard: He cast away the bodily garment many months ago. Last year, the old camel-herder came here after the month of Saavan. The Sarangiya and he were camping in the desert together, when one night a mighty sandstorm arose. It blew all night. It was the kind of gale that uproots khejri trees and sweeps away entire dhanis. The sand swirled and covered the patient camels and forced them to rise on their long legs. The next morning, it was still blowing in full force. But the Sarangiya said he must leave. He needed to be by the tree in six days, before the full moon night, and couldn't be delayed. The old Rabari tried to stop him, but he just laughed. 'I am the sandstorm's favourite playmate,' he said, and walked out with his cloth bundle and sarangi. The storm subsided after three nights and two days and the Rabari continued his trek through the desert. A couple of days before the full moon, he found the Sarangiya's cloth bundle, his still-full water gourd and his faithful sarangi on the desert trail. He searched everywhere but couldn't find the Sarangiya. The storm had buried him somewhere under a sand-tower as she is wont to do with her favourite playmates. The Rabari burned the bundle on a pyre of dried cactus and thorn, and brought the sarangi over.

SSP: You're claiming that the Sarangiya came back from the dead that night and played the sarangi?

Guard: No, Hukum, not just that night. Night after night, Collector Saheb and he played jugalbandis of beauty and pain, longing and fulfilment. The desert and the sky shivered with pleasure. I saw all from my vantage point as the keeper of the gates. He had been here ever since the Rabari brought the sarangi. But he left the other night when even the sarangi gave up and its strings broke. I haven't seen him since.

SSP: I am warning you, Guard. I will forget your white hair and let Thanedaar Saheb take you to his thana. He will burn chillies under you and the truth will flow out along with tears and blood.

Guard: This is the truth, Hukum. That night, the Sarangiya's sarangi finally gave way, his pain was beyond bearing even for the dead wood and leather. Saheb cried as he played his flute, and then the shadows under the tree deepened and I, even I, could see no more – neither Saheb nor the Sarangiya were there when the moon set and the shadows lifted. You can get my skin flayed, but I won't be able to tell you anything different.

I note that the guard has firmly adhered to his statement through several rounds of questioning. He is well past the superannuation age but has been allowed to stay on at the Circuit House. He has no living family and is considered to be some sort of sage or renunciate by the desert folk. They bring their children and their cattle to be blessed by him. According to the statements of the staff of both the Circuit House and the tehsil, he was very attached to the DC. It does not appear that he had any reason to harm the DC or protect anyone who may have harmed him.

The SHO has conducted a thorough investigation and interrogated villagers and known troublemakers from around the tehsil. However, no leads have emerged. The villagers have spoken of the DC's concern for their well-being, how he transported a sick child or camel calf in his jeep to the district hospital, resolved khasra or ownership issues, granted aid in cases of crop failure and other hardships. The tehsil staff were not so satisfied with him, particularly in the last few months, since he had ordered an audit of revenue receipts. However, no one seems to bear a personal grudge against the DC. No strangers were reported in the area on the night of his disappearance, and all of the DC's belongings have been found intact in the Circuit House. The DC's orderly has confirmed that neither his shoes nor his warm clothes were missing. A forensic analysis of the objects sent to the laboratory has revealed nothing of significance either. The mystery surrounding the disappearance of the DC has drawn much adverse attention from newspapers, and the DC's friends in the capital have made allegations of bungling on the part of the investigating officer. I can categorically state that the SHO carried out the investigation very competently. As of now, the cook and the Tehsildar – who is now not in a condition that permits further interrogation – remain principal suspects in the investigation. However, no evidence of any kind linking them to the DC's disappearance has surfaced. The absence of meaningful leads, evidence or motive for foul play has frustrated the investigation into the DC's disappearance.

Now, I come to the second, and in many ways more concerning, part of the matter. On the day after my arrival at the

Circuit House, I had summoned the lambardars, the panches and khedapatis of the village folk to discuss the dispersal of their people. I found them to be obstinate about continuing prayers around the tree – the site where the DC was last seen. Despite being told that they were on government property without due permission and could be jailed for the offence, they maintained that they could not leave until the seven-day period of sthapan – establishing the god in his abode – was complete. After much consideration, and given only five more days of this arbitrary period remained, I permitted them to continue their prayers in the interest of a peaceful dispersion of the gathered crowds. They assured me that they would leave thereafter. I included this in my preliminary report on the DC's disappearance. I continue to believe that it was the right decision at the time, in view of the sensitive nature of the situation, with the chief administrative officer of the district untraceable and religious fervour running high among the gathered villagers. This decision was endorsed by the Range DIG as well as the IG.

However, the seventh day came and went with people continuing to pour into the Circuit House. The village heads proved completely ineffective. The tehsil officials, too, did not seem to have any influence over the villagers. The crowd created a two-fold concern: continued unnecessary focus on the investigations, as well as encroachment of government property. Over time, the villagers constructed a makeshift structure under the tree in the Circuit House compound and some nomads began presiding as priests of the so-called Sukaal Dev residing in the tree. The situation was further aggravated when the Tehsildar, whom I finally persuaded to leave the Circuit House and go to his own home, succumbed to a complete nervous breakdown. The circumstances of the Tehsildar's breakdown are worth a brief mention. On the second or third day after the Tehsildar had left, the constables posted around the Circuit House saw him running wildly towards the compound, shrieking in apparent terror. They tried to restrain him, but he threw himself on the ground before the tree, foaming at the mouth, begging Sukaal Dev to save him from some pret, the local term for an evil spirit. He had to be admitted to the mental hospital in Jaipur, where he remains as of writing this report. I understand a voluntary retirement application has been moved on his behalf. The nervous breakdown of the Tehsildar had an adverse impact from the point of view of the crowd situation. Village folk took it as a sign of Sukaal Dev's potency, and the absurd story was carried in several regional and national newspapers. In consultation with the tehsil and district officials, I made a recommendation to defer forceful crowd dispersal measures until the beginning of the rains. The reasoning was that the village folk would return to their homes for agricultural work which would commence with the rains. The recommendation was accepted by the new DC, and I accordingly instructed my

SHO to discourage the villagers from gathering in numbers but refrain from using force.

In July, the DC alerted us that the situation had not improved despite the rains arriving earlier than usual. It was impossible to use the Circuit House for official purposes due to the constant flow of people. I sent a unit to clear the crowds immediately. After a mild lathi charge, it was reported that the crowds had dispersed. The SHO secured the Circuit House and placed constables at the gate and around the periphery wall. However, a few weeks later, the villagers began trickling back. The constables were unable to prevent them from entering and, in fact, they joined in the prayers, a few of them claiming they heard the DC's flute at dusk. My SHO cleared the area again, this time driving the nomads and villagers in tractor trolleys to the border of the tehsil, and posted fresh guards. This cycle was repeated a few times and the DC called a meeting. By this time, it was clear that radical measures would be necessary to reclaim the Circuit House. The tree was the focal point of the villagers' gatherings, and the only way to resolve the situation was to cut it. Once it was cut, the crowds would have no anchor. Therefore, at the meeting, I made the suggestion that the permanent solution to the encroachment and law-and-order issue would be to cut the tree. The proposal was duly approved by the DC and submitted to the Chief Secretary. Upon receiving approvals, I took charge of the operation. In order to avoid any local issues, labour from a neighbouring state was ferried to the tehsil, the structure under the tree cleared, and the tree itself brought down overnight. The timber was transported to the district headquarters for use in the ongoing construction work at the Collector's bungalow. There was some trouble caused by villagers over the next couple of days when they learnt about the tree. A number of them came wailing to the Circuit House. However, my men were prepared and they were not allowed to congregate. The operation thus concluded smoothly and order was restored in the area.

I note that, until this stage, there was no word of anything untoward happening at the canal works. The first reports arrived three days after the cutting of the tree, suggesting that the water level in the canal was falling rapidly. As is well known by now, the canal ran completely dry in two weeks' time. I inspected the canal and can confirm that no signs of sabotage were found. I understand that the Chief Engineer himself has surveyed the canal site along with a team of geologists and hydrologists, and a technical report has been presented. I note that the report does not identify any causal relationship between the cutting of the tree and the depletion of the underground water, as has been maliciously suggested by newspapers. On the contrary, the report suggests that the likely cause of the canal drying up is the underground water escaping through some subterranean crack in the bedrock.

I would like to conclude this report with a confirmation that all departmental protocols have been followed in making decisions regarding the situation at the Circuit House, and approvals given by senior state officials have been duly documented in official files.

Acknowledgements

That this book got written and published is due to those who supported me in various ways in my solitary and self-doubt filled pursuit: friends Som, Manish, Siddhartha, Gunjan who encouraged, believed and advised with astonishing generosity; Priti Gill and Ravi Singh who showed faith in my writing at an early stage; my editor Rahul Soni, without whose advice and encouragement neither *Daura* nor *Bhaunri* would have taken their present form; my publisher Udayan Mitra, whose warmth and engagement made the journey from manuscript to published book memorable; my father Dr Surendra Upadhyay, who gave me all my words, and mother Puja Upadhyay, who gave all of herself; my father-in-law and mother-in-law, Krishan Kumar Sharma and Girija Sharma, my sister, sisters-in-law, brothers-in-law, nieces, nephews, cousins, who created an affectionate and nurturing environment; my husband Vikas and son Yashodhar, who enhance me in ways I cannot describe. Towards all of them, my gratitude is unbounded, inexpressible, wordless.